Bret Harte

A Sappho of Green Springs and other stories

Bret Harte

A Sappho of Green Springs and other stories

ISBN/EAN: 9783744749343

Printed in Europe, USA, Canada, Australia, Japan

Cover: Foto ©Andreas Hilbeck / pixelio.de

More available books at **www.hansebooks.com**

A SAPPHO OF GREEN SPRINGS
AND OTHER STORIES

BY

BRET HARTE

BOSTON AND NEW YORK
HOUGHTON, MIFFLIN AND COMPANY
The Riverside Press, Cambridge
1891

The Riverside Press, Cambridge, Mass., U. S. A.
Electrotyped and Printed by H. O. Houghton & Co.

CONTENTS.

———•—·

A SAPPHO OF GREEN SPRINGS.

CHAPTER I.

"Come in," said the editor.

The door of the editorial room of the "Excelsior Magazine" began to creak painfully under the hesitating pressure of an uncertain and unfamiliar hand. This continued until with a start of irritation the editor faced directly about, throwing his leg over the arm of his chair with a certain youthful dexterity. With one hand gripping its back, the other still grasping a proof-slip, and his pencil in his mouth, he stared at the intruder.

The stranger, despite his hesitating entrance, did not seem in the least disconcerted. He was a tall man, looking even taller by reason of the long formless overcoat he wore, known as a "duster," and by a long straight beard that depended from his chin, which he combed with two reflective fingers as he contemplated the editor. The red dust which still lay in the creases of his garment and in the curves of his soft felt hat, and left a dusty circle like a precipitated halo around his feet, proclaimed him, if not a countryman, a recent inland importation by coach. " Busy ? " he said, in a grave but pleasant voice. " I kin wait. Don't mind *me.* Go on."

The editor indicated a chair with his disengaged hand and plunged again into his proof-slips. The stranger surveyed the scant furniture and appointments of the office with a look of grave curiosity, and then, taking a chair, fixed an earnest, penetrating gaze on the editor's profile. The editor felt it, and, without looking up, said : —

" Well, go on."

" But you 're busy. I kin wait."

" I shall not be less busy this morning. I can listen."

" I want you to give me the name of a certain person who writes in your magazine."

The editor's eye glanced at the second right-hand drawer of his desk. It did not contain the names of his contributors, but what in the traditions of his office was accepted as an equivalent, — a revolver. He had never yet presented either to an inquirer. But he laid aside his proofs, and, with a slight darkening of his youthful, discontented face, said, " What do you want to know for ? "

The question was so evidently unexpected that the stranger's face colored slightly, and he hesitated. The editor meanwhile, without taking his eyes from the man, mentally ran over the contents of the last magazine. They had been of a singularly peaceful character. There seemed to be nothing to justify homicide on his part or the stranger's. Yet there was no knowing, and his questioner's bucolic appearance by no means precluded an assault. Indeed, it had been a legend of the office that a predecessor had suffered vicariously from a geological hammer covertly introduced into a scientific controversy by an irate professor.

" As we make ourselves responsible for the conduct of the magazine," continued the young editor, with mature severity, " we do not give up the names of our contributors. If you do not agree with their opinions " —

" But I *do*," said the stranger, with his former composure, " and I reckon that 's why I want to know who wrote those verses called ' Underbrush,' signed ' White Violet,' in your last number. They 're pow'ful pretty."

The editor flushed slightly, and glanced instinctively around for any unexpected witness of his ludicrous mistake. The fear of ridicule was uppermost in his mind, and he was more relieved at his mistake not being overheard than at its groundlessness.

"The verses *are* pretty," he said, recovering himself, with a critical air, "and I am glad you like them. But even then, you know, I could not give you the lady's name without her permission. I will write to her and ask it, if you like."

The actual fact was that the verses had been sent to him anonymously from a remote village in the Coast Range, — the address being the post-office and the signature initials.

The stranger looked disturbed. "Then she ain't about here anywhere?" he said, with a vague gesture. "She don't belong to the office?"

The young editor beamed with tolerant superiority: "No, I am sorry to say."

"I should like to have got to see her and kinder asked her a few questions," continued the stranger, with the same reflective seriousness. "You see, it wasn't just the rhymin' o' them verses, — and they kinder sing themselves to ye, don't they? — it was n't the chyce o' words, — and I reckon they allus hit the idee in the centre shot every time, — it was n't the ideas and moral she sort o' drew out o' what she was tellin', — but it was the straight thing itself, — the truth!"

"The truth?" repeated the editor.

"Yes, sir. I 've bin there. I 've seen all that she's seen in the brush — the little flicks and checkers o' light and shadder down in the brown dust that you wonder how it ever got through the dark of the woods, and that allus seems to slip away like a snake or a lizard if you grope. I 've heard all that she's heard there — the creepin', the sighin', and the whisperin' through the bracken and the ground-vines of all that lives there."

"You seem to be a poet yourself," said the editor, with a patronizing smile.

"I 'm a lumberman, up in Mendocino," returned the stranger, with sublime *naïveté.* "Got a mill there. You see, sightin' standin' timber and selectin' from the gen'ral show of the trees in the ground and the lay of roots hez sorter made me take notice." He paused. "Then," he added, somewhat despondingly, "you don't know who she is?"

" No," said the editor, reflectively ; " not even if it is really a *woman* who writes."

" Eh ? "

" Well, you see, ' White Violet ' may as well be the *nom de plume* of a man as of a woman, especially if adopted for the purpose of mystification. The handwriting, I remember, was more boyish than feminine."

" No," returned the stranger doggedly, " it was n't no *man*. There 's ideas and words there that only come from a woman : baby-talk to the birds, you know, and a kind of fearsome keer of bugs and creepin' things that don't come to a man who wears boots and trousers. Well," he added, with a re-turn to his previous air of resigned disap-pointment, " I suppose you don't even know what she 's like ? "

" No," responded the editor, cheerfully. Then, following an idea suggested by the odd mingling of sentiment and shrewd per-ception in the man before him, he added : " Probably not at all like anything you im-agine. She may be a mother with three or four children ; or an old maid who keeps a boarding-house ; or a wrinkled school-mis-tress ; or a chit of a school-girl. I 've had some fair verses from a red-haired girl of fourteen at the Seminary," he concluded with professional coolness.

The stranger regarded him with the naïve wonder of an inexperienced man. Having paid this tribute to his superior knowledge, he regained his previous air of grave perception. " I reckon she ain't none of them. But I 'm keepin' you from your work. Goodby. My name 's Bowers — Jim Bowers, of Mendocino. If you 're up my way, give me a call. And if you do write to this yer 'White Violet,' and she 's willin', send me her address."

He shook the editor's hand warmly — even in its literal significance of imparting a good deal of his own earnest caloric to the editor's fingers — and left the room. His footfall echoed along the passage and died out, and with it, I fear, all impression of his visit from the editor's mind, as he plunged again into the silent task before him.

Presently he was conscious of a melodious humming and a light leisurely step at the entrance of the hall. They continued on in an easy harmony and unaffected as the passage of a bird. Both were pleasant and both familiar to the editor. They belonged to Jack Hamlin, by vocation a gambler, by taste a musician, on his way from his apartments on the upper floor, where he had just risen, to drop into his friend's editorial room and glance over the exchanges, as was his habit before breakfast.

The door opened lightly. The editor was conscious of a faint odor of scented soap, a sensation of freshness and cleanliness, the impression of a soft hand like a woman's on his shoulder and, like a woman's, momentarily and playfully caressing, the passage of a graceful shadow across his desk, and the next moment Jack Hamlin was ostentatiously dusting a chair with an open newspaper preparatory to sitting down.

"You ought to ship that office-boy of yours, if he can't keep things cleaner," he said, suspending his melody to eye grimly the dust which Mr. Bowers had shaken from his departing feet.

The editor did not look up until he had finished revising a difficult paragraph. By that time Mr. Hamlin had comfortably settled himself on a cane sofa, and, possibly out of deference to his surroundings, had subdued his song to a peculiarly low, soft, and heart-breaking whistle as he unfolded a newspaper. Clean and faultless in his appearance, he had the rare gift of being able to get up at two in the afternoon with much of the dewy freshness and all of the moral superiority of an early riser.

"You ought to have been here just now, Jack," said the editor.

"Not a row, old man, eh?" inquired Jack, with a faint accession of interest.

"No," said the editor, smiling. Then he related the incidents of the previous interview, with a certain humorous exaggeration which was part of his nature. But Jack did not smile.

"You ought to have booted him out of the ranch on sight," he said. "What right had he to come here prying into a lady's affairs? — at least a lady as far as *he* knows. Of course she's some old blowzy with frumpled hair trying to rope in a greenhorn with a string of words and phrases," concluded Jack, carelessly, who had an equally cynical distrust of the sex and of literature.

"That's about what I told him," said the editor.

"That's just what you *should n't* have told him," returned Jack. "You ought to have stuck up for that woman as if she'd been your own mother. Lord! you fellows don't know how to run a magazine. You ought to let *me* sit on that chair and tackle your customers."

"What would you have done, Jack?" asked the editor, much amused to find that his hitherto invincible hero was not above the ordinary human weakness of offering advice as to editorial conduct.

"Done?" reflected Jack. "Well, first, sonny, I should n't keep a revolver in a drawer that I had to *open* to get at."

"But what would you have said?"

"I should simply have asked him what was the price of lumber at Mendocino," said Jack, sweetly, "and when he told me, I should have said that the samples he was offering out of his own head would n't suit. You see, you don't want any trifling in such matters. You write well enough, my boy," continued he, turning over his paper, "but what you're lacking in is editorial dignity. But go on with your work. Don't mind me."

Thus admonished, the editor again bent over his desk, and his friend softly took up his suspended song. The editor had not proceeded far in his corrections when Jack's voice again broke the silence.

" Where are those d—d verses, anyway?"

Without looking up, the editor waved his pencil towards an uncut copy of the " Excelsior Magazine " lying on the table.

" You don't suppose I 'm going to *read* them, do you?" said Jack, aggrievedly. " Why don't you say what they 're about? That 's your business as editor."

But that functionary, now wholly lost and wandering in the *non-sequitur* of an involved passage in the proof before him, only waved an impatient remonstrance with his pencil and knit his brows. Jack, with a sigh, took up the magazine.

A long silence followed, broken only by the hurried rustling of sheets of copy and an occasional exasperated start from the editor. The sun was already beginning to slant a dusty beam across his desk; Jack's whistling had long since ceased. Presently, with an exclamation of relief, the editor laid aside the last proof-sheet and looked up.

Jack Hamlin had closed the magazine, but with one hand thrown over the back of the sofa he was still holding it, his slim forefinger between its leaves to keep the place, and his handsome profile and dark lashes lifted towards the window. The editor, smiling at this unwonted abstraction, said, quietly, —

"Well, what do you think of them?"

Jack rose, laid the magazine down, settled his white waistcoat with both hands, and lounged towards his friend with audacious but slightly veiled and shining eyes. "They sort of sing themselves to you," he said, quietly, leaning beside the editor's desk, and looking down upon him. After a pause he said, "Then you don't know what she's like?"

"That's what Mr. Bowers asked me," remarked the editor.

"D—n Bowers!"

"I suppose you also wish me to write and ask for permission to give you her address?" said the editor, with great gravity.

"No," said Jack, coolly. "I propose to give it to *you* within a week, and you will pay me with a breakfast. I should like to have it said that I was once a paid contributor to literature. If I don't give it to you, I'll stand you a dinner, that's all."

"Done!" said the editor. "And you know nothing of her now?"

"No," said Jack, promptly. "Nor you?"

"No more than I have told you."

"That 'll do. So long!" And Jack, carefully adjusting his glossy hat over his curls at an ominously wicked angle, sauntered lightly from the room. The editor, glancing after his handsome figure and hearing him take up his pretermitted whistle as he passed out, began to think that the contingent dinner was by no means an inevitable prospect.

Howbeit, he plunged once more into his monotonous duties. But the freshness of the day seemed to have departed with Jack, and the later interruptions of foreman and publisher were of a more practical character. It was not until the post arrived that the superscription on one of the letters caught his eye, and revived his former interest. It was the same hand as that of his unknown contributor's manuscript — ill-formed and boyish. He opened the envelope. It contained another poem with the same signature, but also a note — much longer than the brief lines that accompanied the first contribution — was scrawled upon a separate piece of paper. This the editor opened first, and read the following, with an amazement that for the moment dominated all other sense : —

Mr. Editor, — I see you have got my poetry in. But I don't see the spondulix that oughter follow. Perhaps you don't know where to send it. Then I 'll tell you. Send the money to Lock Box 47, Green Springs P. O., per Wells Fargo's Express, and I 'll get it there, on account of my parents not knowing. We 're very high-toned, and they would think it 's low making poetry for papers. Send amount usually paid for poetry in your papers. Or may be you think I make poetry for nothing? That 's where you slip up!

Yours truly,   White Violet.

P. S. — If you don't pay for poetry, send this back. It 's as good as what you did put in, and is just as hard to make. You hear me? that 's me — all the time.

White Violet.

The editor turned quickly to the new contribution for some corroboration of what he felt must be an extraordinary blunder. But no! The few lines that he hurriedly read breathed the same atmosphere of intellectual repose, gentleness, and imagination as the first contribution. And yet they were in the same handwriting as the singular missive, and both were identical with the previous manuscript.

Had he been the victim of a hoax, and were the verses not original? No; they were distinctly original, local in color, and even local in the use of certain old English words that were common in the Southwest. He had before noticed the apparent incongruity of the handwriting and the text, and it was possible that for the purposes of disguise the poet might have employed an amanuensis. But how could he reconcile the incongruity of the mercenary and slangy purport of the missive itself with the mental habit of its author? Was it possible that these inconsistent qualities existed in the one individual? He smiled grimly as he thought of his visitor Bowers and his friend Jack. He was startled as he remembered the purely imaginative picture he had himself given to the seriously interested Bowers of the possible incongruous personality of the poetess.

Was he quite fair in keeping this from Jack? Was it really honorable, in view of their wager? It is to be feared that a very human enjoyment of Jack's possible discomfiture quite as much as any chivalrous friendship impelled the editor to ring eventually for the office-boy.

"See if Mr. Hamlin is in his rooms."

The editor then sat down, and wrote rapidly as follows: —

DEAR MADAM, — You are as right as you are generous in supposing that only ignorance of your address prevented the manager from previously remitting the honorarium for your beautiful verses. He now begs to send it to you in the manner you have indicated. As the verses have attracted deserved attention, I have been applied to for your address. Should you care to submit it to me to be used at my discretion, I shall feel honored by your confidence. But this is a matter left entirely to your own kindness and better judgment. Meantime, I take pleasure in accepting "White Violet's" present contribution, and remain, dear madam, your obedient servant,

THE EDITOR.

The boy returned as he was folding the letter. Mr. Hamlin was not only *not* in his rooms, but, according to his negro servant Pete, had left town an hour ago for a few days in the country.

"Did he say where?" asked the editor, quickly.

"No, sir : he did n't know."

"Very well. Take this to the manager." He addressed the letter, and, scrawling a few hieroglyphics on a memorandum-tag, tore it off, and handed it with the letter to the boy.

An hour later he stood in the manager's office. "The next number is pretty well made up," he said, carelessly, "and I think of taking a day or two off."

"Certainly," said the manager. "It will do you good. Where do you think you 'll go?"

"I have n't quite made up my mind."

CHAPTER II.

" HULLO ! " said Jack Hamlin.

He had halted his mare at the edge of an abrupt chasm. It did not appear to be fifty feet across, yet its depth must have been nearly two hundred to where the hidden mountain-stream, of which it was the banks, alternately slipped, tumbled, and fell with murmuring and monotonous regularity. One or two pine-trees growing on the opposite edge, loosened at the roots, had tilted their straight shafts like spears over the abyss, and the top of one, resting on the upper branches of a sycamore a few yards from him, served as an aerial bridge for the passage of a boy of fourteen to whom Mr. Hamlin's challenge was addressed.

The boy stopped midway in his perilous transit, and, looking down upon the horseman, responded, coolly, " Hullo, yourself ! "

" Is that the only way across this infernal hole, or the one you prefer for exercise ? " continued Hamlin, gravely.

The boy sat down on a bough, allowing his bare feet to dangle over the dizzy depths, and critically examined his questioner. Jack had on this occasion modified his usual correct conventional attire by a tasteful combination of a vaquero's costume, and, in loose white bullion-fringed trousers, red sash, jacket, and sombrero, looked infinitely more dashing and picturesque than his original. Nevertheless, the boy did not reply. Mr. Hamlin's pride in his usual ascendency over women, children, horses, and all unreasoning animals was deeply nettled. He smiled, however, and said, quietly, —

"Come here, George Washington. I want to talk to you."

Without rejecting this august yet impossible title, the boy presently lifted his feet, and carelessly resumed his passage across the chasm until, reaching the sycamore, he began to let himself down squirrel-wise, leap by leap, with an occasional trapeze swinging from bough to bough, dropping at last easily to the ground. Here he appeared to be rather good-looking, albeit the sun and air had worked a miracle of brown tan and freckles on his exposed surfaces, until the mottling of his oval cheeks looked like a

polished bird's egg. Indeed, it struck Mr.
Hamlin that he was as intensely a part of
that sylvan seclusion as the hidden brook
that murmured, the brown velvet shadows
that lay like trappings on the white flanks
of his horse, the quivering heat, and the
stinging spice of bay. Mr. Hamlin had
vague ideas of dryads and fauns, but at that
moment would have bet something on the
chances of their survival.

"I did not hear what you said just now,
general," he remarked, with great elegance
of manner, "but I know from your reputation that it could not be a lie. I therefore
gather that there *is* another way across."

The boy smiled; rather, his very short
upper lip apparently vanished completely
over his white teeth, and his very black
eyes, which showed a great deal of the white
around them, danced in their orbits.

"But *you* could n't find it," he said, slyly.

"No more could you find the half-dollar I
dropped just now, unless I helped you."

Mr. Hamlin, by way of illustration, leaned
deeply over his left stirrup, and pointed to
the ground. At the same moment a bright
half-dollar absolutely appeared to glitter in
the herbage at the point of his finger. It

was a trick that had always brought great pleasure and profit to his young friends, and some loss and discomfiture of wager to his older ones.

The boy picked up the coin: "There's a dip and a level crossing about a mile over yer," — he pointed, — "but it's through the woods, and they're that high with thick bresh."

"With what?"

"Bresh," repeated the boy; "*that*," — pointing to a few fronds of bracken growing in the shadow of the sycamore.

"Oh! underbrush?"

"Yes; I said 'bresh,'" returned the boy, doggedly. "*You* might get through, ef you war spry, but not your hoss. Where do you want to go, anyway?"

"Do you know, George," said Mr. Hamlin, lazily throwing his right leg over the horn of his saddle for greater ease and deliberation in replying, "it's very odd, but that's just what *I'd* like to know. Now, what would *you*, in your broad statesmanlike views of things generally, advise?"

Quite convinced of the stranger's mental unsoundness, the boy glanced again at his half-dollar, as if to make sure of its integrity, pocketed it doubtfully, and turned away.

"Where are you going?" said Hamlin, resuming his seat with the agility of a circus-rider, and spurring forward.

"To Green Springs, where I live, two miles over the ridge on the far slope," — indicating the direction.

"Ah!" said Jack, with thoughtful gravity. "Well, kindly give my love to your sister, will you?"

"George Washington did n't have no sister," said the boy, cunningly.

"Can I have been mistaken?" said Hamlin, lifting his hand to his forehead with grieved accents. "Then it seems *you* have. Kindly give her my love."

"Which one?" asked the boy, with a swift glance of mischief. "I 've got four."

"The one that 's like you," returned Hamlin, with prompt exactitude. "Now, where 's the 'bresh' you spoke of?"

"Keep along the edge until you come to the log-slide. Foller that, and it 'll lead you into the woods. But ye won't go far, I tell ye. When you have to turn back, instead o' comin' back here, you kin take the trail that goes round the woods, and that 'll bring ye out into the stage road ag'in near the post-office at the Green Springs crossin' and the new hotel. That 'll be war ye 'll turn up, I reckon," he added, reflectively. "Fellers that come yer gunnin' and fishin' gin'rally do," he concluded, with a half-inquisitive air.

"Ah?" said Mr. Hamlin, quietly shedding the inquiry. "Green Springs Hotel is where the stage stops, eh?"

"Yes, and at the post-office," said the boy. "She 'll be along here soon," he added.

"If you mean the Santa Cruz stage," said Hamlin, "she 's here already. I passed her on the ridge half an hour ago."

The boy gave a sudden start, and a quick uneasy expression passed over his face. "Go 'long with ye!" he said, with a forced smile: "it ain't her time yet."

"But I *saw* her," repeated Hamlin, much amused. "Are you expecting company? Hullo! Where are you off to? Come back."

But his companion had already vanished in the thicket with the undeliberate and impulsive act of an animal. There was a momentary rustle in the alders fifty feet away, and then all was silent. The hidden brook

took up its monotonous murmur, the tapping
of a distant woodpecker became suddenly
audible, and Mr. Hamlin was again alone.

" Wonder whether he 's got parents in the
stage, and has been playing truant here," he
mused, lazily. " Looked as if he 'd been
up to some devilment, or more like as if he
was primed for it. If he 'd been a little
older, I 'd have bet he was in league with
some road-agents to watch the coach. Just
my luck to have him light out as I was beginning to get some talk out of him." He
paused, looked at his watch, and straightened himself in his stirrups. " Four o'clock.
I reckon I might as well try the woods and
what that imp calls the ' bresh ; ' I may
strike a shanty or a native by the way."

With this determination, Mr. Hamlin
urged his horse along the faint trail by the
brink of the watercourse which the boy had
just indicated. He had no definite end in
view beyond the one that had brought him
the day before to that locality — his quest
of the unknown poetess. His clue would
have seemed to ordinary humanity the faintest. He had merely noted the provincial
name of a certain plant mentioned in the
poem, and learned that its *habitat* was lim-

ited to the southern local range ; while its peculiar nomenclature was clearly of French Creole or Gulf State origin. This gave him a large though sparsely-populated area for locality, while it suggested a settlement of Louisianians or Mississippians near the Summit, of whom, through their native gambling proclivities, he was professionally cognizant. But he mainly trusted Fortune. Secure in his faith in the feminine character of that goddess, he relied a great deal on her well-known weakness for scamps of his quality.

It was not long before he came to the "slide" — a lightly-cut or shallow ditch. It descended slightly in a course that was far from straight, at times diverging to avoid the obstacles of trees or boulders, at times shaving them so closely as to leave smooth abrasions along their sides made by the grinding passage of long logs down the incline. The track itself was slippery from this, and pre-occupied all Hamlin's skill as a horseman, even to the point of stopping his usual careless whistle. At the end of half an hour the track became level again, and he was confronted with a singular phenomenon.

He had entered the wood, and the trail

seemed to cleave through a far-stretching, motionless sea of ferns that flowed on either side to the height of his horse's flanks. The straight shafts of the trees rose like columns from their hidden bases and were lost again in a roof of impenetrable leafage, leaving a clear space of fifty feet between, through which the surrounding horizon of sky was perfectly visible. All the light that entered this vast sylvan hall came from the sides; nothing permeated from above; nothing radiated from below; the height of the crest on which the wood was placed gave it this lateral illumination, but gave it also the profound isolation of some temple raised by long-forgotten hands. In spite of the height of these clear shafts, they seemed dwarfed by the expanse of the wood, and in the farthest perspective the base of ferns and the capital of foliage appeared almost to meet. As the boy had warned him, the slide had turned aside, skirting the wood to follow the incline, and presently the little trail he now followed vanished utterly, leaving him and his horse adrift breast-high in this green and yellow sea of fronds. But Mr. Hamlin, imperious of obstacles, and touched by some curiosity, continued to advance lazily, taking the bearings of a larger red-wood in the centre of the grove for his objective point. The elastic mass gave way before him, brushing his knees or combing his horse's flanks with wide-spread elfin fingers, and closing up behind him as he passed, as if to obliterate any track by which he might return. Yet his usual luck did not desert him here. Being on horseback, he found that he could detect what had been invisible to the boy and probably to all pedestrians, namely, that the growth was not equally dense, that there were certain thinner and more open spaces that he could take advantage of by more circuitous progression, always, however, keeping the bearings of the central tree. This he at last reached, and halted his panting horse. Here a new idea which had been haunting him since he entered the wood took fuller possession of him. He had seen or known all this before! There was a strange familiarity either in these objects or in the impression or spell they left upon him. He remembered the verses! Yes, this was the " underbrush " which the poetess had described : the gloom above and below, the light that seemed blown through it like the wind, the suggestion of hidden life beneath this tangled luxuriance, which she alone had penetrated, — all this was here. But, more than that, here was the atmosphere that she had breathed into the plaintive melody of her verse. It did not necessarily follow that Mr. Hamlin's translation of her sentiment was the correct one, or that the ideas her verses had provoked in his mind were at all what had been hers: in his easy susceptibility he was simply thrown into a corresponding mood of emotion and relieved himself with song. One of the verses he had already associated in his mind with the rhythm of an old plantation melody, and it struck his fancy to take advantage of the solitude to try its effect. Humming to himself, at first softly, he at last grew bolder, and let his voice drift away through the stark pillars of the sylvan colonnade till it seemed to suffuse and fill it with no more effort than the light which strayed in on either side. Sitting thus, his hat thrown a little back from his clustering curls, the white neck and shoulders of his horse uplifting him above the crested mass of fern, his red sash the one fleck of color in their olive depths, I am afraid he looked much more like the real minstrel of the

grove than the unknown poetess who trans-
figured it. But this, as has been already indicated, was Jack Hamlin's peculiar gift.
Even as he had previously outshone the
vaquero in his borrowed dress, he now si-
lenced and supplanted a few fluttering blue-
jays — rightful tenants of the wood — with
a more graceful and airy presence and a far
sweeter voice.

The open horizon towards the west had
taken a warmer color from the already slanting sun when Mr. Hamlin, having rested his
horse, turned to that direction. He had noticed that the wood was thinner there, and,
pushing forward, he was presently rewarded
by the sound of far-off wheels, and knew he
must be near the high-road that the boy had
spoken of. Having given up his previous
intention of crossing the stream, there seemed
nothing better for him to do than to follow
the truant's advice and take the road back
to Green Springs. Yet he was loath to
leave the wood, halting on its verge, and
turning to look back into its charmed re-
cesses. Once or twice — perhaps because he
recalled the words of the poem — that yel-
lowish sea of ferns had seemed instinct with
hidden life, and he had even fancied, here

and there, a swaying of its plumed crests. Howbeit, he still lingered long enough for the open sunlight into which he had obtruded to point out the bravery of his handsome figure. Then he wheeled his horse, the light glanced from polished double bit and bridle-fripperies, caught his red sash and bullion buttons, struck a parting flash from his silver spurs, and he was gone!

For a moment the light streamed unbrokenly through the wood. And then it could be seen that the yellow mass of undergrowth *had* moved with the passage of another figure than his own. For ever since he had entered the shade, a woman, shawled in a vague, shapeless fashion, had watched him wonderingly, eagerly, excitedly, gliding from tree to tree as he advanced, or else dropping breathlessly below the fronds of fern whence she gazed at him as between parted fingers. When he wheeled she had run openly to the west, albeit with hidden face and still clinging shawl, and taken a last look at his retreating figure. And then, with a faint but lingering sigh, she drew back into the shadow of the wood again and vanished also.

CHAPTER III.

AT the end of twenty minutes Mr. Hamlin reined in his mare. He had just observed in the distant shadows of a by-lane that intersected his road the vanishing flutter of two light print dresses. Without a moment's hesitation he lightly swerved out of the high-road and followed the retreating figures.

As he neared them, they seemed to be two slim young girls, evidently so preoccupied with the rustic amusement of edging each other off the grassy border into the dust of the track that they did not perceive his approach. Little shrieks, slight scufflings, and interjections of " Cynthy! you limb!" " Quit that, Eunice, now!" and " I just call that real mean!" apparently drowned the sound of his canter in the soft dust. Checking his speed to a gentle trot, and pressing his horse close beside the opposite fence, he passed them with gravely uplifted hat and a serious, preoccupied air.

But in that single, seemingly conventional glance, Mr. Hamlin had seen that they were both pretty, and that one had the short upper lip of his errant little guide. A hundred yards farther on he halted, as if irresolutely, gazed doubtfully ahead of him, and then turned back. An expression of innocent — almost childlike — concern was clouding the rascal's face. It was well, as the two girls had drawn closely together, having been apparently surprised in the midst of a glowing eulogium of this glorious passing vision by its sudden return. At his nearer approach, the one with the short upper lip hid that piquant feature and the rest of her rosy face behind the other's shoulder, which was suddenly and significantly opposed to the advance of this handsōme intruder, with a certain dignity, half real, half affected, but wholly charming. The protectress appeared — possibly from her defensive attitude — the superior of her companion.

Audacious as Jack was to his own sex, he had early learned that such rare but discomposing graces as he possessed required a certain apologetic attitude when presented to women, and that it was only a plain man who could be always complacently self-confident in their presence. There was, consequently, a hesitating lowering of this hypo-crite's brown eyelashes as he said, in almost pained accents, —

"Excuse me, but I fear I 've taken the wrong road. I 'm going to Green Springs."

"I reckon you 've taken the wrong road, wherever you 're going," returned the young lady, having apparently made up her mind to resent each of Jack's perfections as a separate impertinence : "this is a *private* road." She drew herself fairly up here, although gurgled at in the ear and pinched in the arm by her companion.

"I beg your pardon," said Jack, meekly. "I see I 'm trespassing on your grounds. I 'm very sorry. Thank you for telling me. I should have gone on a mile or two farther, I suppose, until I came to your house," he added, innocently.

"A mile or two ! You 'd have run chock ag'in' our gate in another minit," said the short-lipped one, eagerly. But a sharp nudge from her companion sent her back again into cover, where she waited expectantly for another crushing retort from her protector.

But, alas! it did not come. One cannot

be always witty, and Jack looked distressed. Nevertheless, he took advantage of the pause.

"It was so stupid in me, as I think your brother" — looking at Short-lip — "very carefully told me the road."

The two girls darted quick glances at each other. "Oh, Bawb!" said the first speaker, in wearied accents, — "*that* limb! He don't keer."

"But he *did* care," said Hamlin, quietly, "and gave me a good deal of information. Thanks to him, I was able to see that ferny wood that's so famous — about two miles up the road. You know — the one that there's a poem written about!"

The shot told! Short-lip burst into a display of dazzling little teeth and caught the other girl convulsively by the shoulders. The superior girl bent her pretty brows, and said, "Eunice, what's gone of ye? Quit that!" but, as Hamlin thought, paled slightly.

"Of course," said Hamlin, quickly, "you know — the poem everybody's talking about. Dear me! let me see! how does it go?" The rascal knit his brows, said, "Ah, yes," and then murmured the verse he had lately sung quite as musically.

Short-lip was shamelessly exalted and excited. Really she could scarcely believe it! She already heard herself relating the whole occurrence. Here was the most beautiful young man she had ever seen — an entire stranger — talking to them in the most beautiful and natural way, right in the lane, and reciting poetry to her sister! It was like a novel — only more so. She thought that Cynthia, on the other hand, looked distressed, and — she must say it — " silly."

All of which Jack noted, and was wise. He had got all he wanted — at present. He gathered up his reins.

" Thank you so much, and your brother, too, Miss Cynthia," he said, without looking up. Then, adding, with a parting glance and smile, " But don't tell Bob how stupid I was," he swiftly departed.

In half an hour he was at the Green Springs Hotel. As he rode into the stable yard, he noticed that the coach had only just arrived, having been detained by a land-slip on the Summit road. With the recollection of Bob fresh in his mind, he glanced at the loungers at the stage office. The boy was not there, but a moment later Jack detected him among the waiting crowd at the post-office opposite. With a view of following up his inquiries, he crossed the road as the boy entered the vestibule of the post-office. He arrived in time to see him unlock one of a row of numbered letter-boxes rented by subscribers, which occupied a partition by the window, and take out a small package and a letter. But in that brief glance Mr. Hamlin detected the printed address of the " Excelsior Magazine " on the wrapper. It was enough. Luck was certainly with him.

He had time to get rid of the wicked sparkle that had lit his dark eyes, and to lounge carelessly towards the boy as the lat- · ter broke open the package, and then hurriedly concealed it in his jacket-pocket, and started for the door. Mr. Hamlin quickly followed him, unperceived, and, as he stepped into the street, gently tapped him on the shoulder. The boy turned and faced him quickly. But Mr. Hamlin's eyes showed nothing but lazy good-humor.

" Hullo, Bob. Where are you going ? "

The boy again looked up suspiciously at this revelation of his name.

" Home," he said, briefly.

" Oh, over yonder," said Hamlin, calmly. " I don't mind walking with you as far as the lane."

He saw the boy's eyes glance furtively towards an alley that ran beside the blacksmith's shop a few rods ahead, and was convinced that he intended to evade him there. Slipping his arm carelessly in the youth's, he concluded to open fire at once.

"Bob," he said, with irresistible gravity, "I did not know when I met you this morning that I had the honor of addressing a poet — none other than the famous author of 'Underbrush.'"

The boy started back, and endeavored to withdraw his arm, but Mr. Hamlin tightened his hold, without, however, changing his careless expression.

"You see," he continued, "the editor is a friend of mine, and, being afraid this package might not get into the right hands — as you did n't give your name — he deputized me to come here and see that it was all square. As you 're rather young, for all you 're so gifted, I reckon I 'd better go home with you, and take a receipt from your parents. That 's about square, I think?"

The consternation of the boy was so evident and so far beyond Mr. Hamlin's expectation that he instantly halted him, gazed into his shifting eyes, and gave a long whistle.

" Who said it was for *me?* Wot you talkin' about? Lemme go!" gasped the boy, with the short intermittent breath of mingled fear and passion.

" Bob," said Mr. Hamlin, in a singularly colorless voice which was very rare with him, and an expression quite unlike his own, " what is your little game?"

The boy looked down in dogged silence.

" Out with it! Who are you playing this on?"

" It's all among my own folks; it's nothin' to *you*," said the boy, suddenly beginning to struggle violently, as if inspired by this extenuating fact.

"Among your own folks, eh? White Violet and the rest, eh? But *she's* not in it?"

No reply.

" Hand me over that package. I'll give it back to you again."

The boy handed it to Mr. Hamlin. He read the letter, and found the inclosure contained a twenty-dollar gold-piece. A half-supercilious smile passed over his face at this revelation of the inadequate emoluments of literature and the trifling inducements to crime. Indeed, I fear the affair began to

take a less serious moral complexion in his
eyes.

" Then White Violet — your sister Cynthia, you know," continued Mr. Hamlin, in
easy parenthesis — " wrote for this ? " holding the coin contemplatively in his fingers,
" and you calculated to nab it yourself ? "

The quick searching glance with which
Bob received the name of his sister, Mr.
Hamlin attributed only to his natural surprise that this stranger should be on such
familiar terms with her ; but the boy responded immediately and bluntly : —

" No ! *She* did n't write for it. She
did n't want nobody to know who she was.
Nobody wrote for it but me. Nobody *knew
folks was paid for po'try but me.* I found
it out from a feller. I wrote for it. *I* was n't
goin' to let that skunk of an editor have it
himself ! "

" And you thought *you* would take it,"
said Hamlin, his voice resuming its old tone.
" Well, George — I mean Bob, your conduct
was praiseworthy, although your intentions
were bad. Still, twenty dollars is rather too
much for your trouble. Suppose we say
five and call it square ? " He handed the
astonished boy five dollars. " Now, George

Washington," he continued, taking four other twenty-dollar pieces from his pocket, and adding them to the inclosure, which he carefully refolded, "I'm going to give you another chance to live up to your reputation. You'll take that package, and hand it to White Violet, and say you found it, just as it is, in the lock-box. I'll keep the letter, for it would knock you endways if it was seen, and I'll make it all right with the editor. But, as I've got to tell him that I've seen White Violet myself, and know she's got it, I expect *you* to manage in some way to have me see her. I'll manage the rest of it; and I won't blow on you, either. You'll come back to the hotel, and tell me what you've done. And now, George," concluded Mr. Hamlin, succeeding at last in fixing the boy's evasive eye with a peculiar look, "it may be just as well for you to understand that I know every nook and corner of this place, that I've already been through that underbrush you spoke of once this morning, and that I've got a mare that can go wherever *you* can, and a d—d sight quicker!"

"I'll give the package to White Violet," said the boy, doggedly.

"And you 'll come back to the hotel?"

The boy hesitated, and then said, "I 'll come back."

"All right, then. *Adios*, general."

Bob disappeared around the corner of a cross-road at a rapid trot, and Mr. Hamlin turned into the hotel.

"Smart little chap that!" he said to the barkeeper.

"You bet!" returned the man, who, having recognized Mr. Hamlin, was delighted at the prospect of conversing with a gentleman of such decidedly dangerous reputation. "But he 's been allowed to run a little wild since old man Delatour died, and the widder 's got enough to do, I reckon, lookin' arter her four gals, and takin' keer of old Delatour's ranch over yonder. I guess it 's pretty hard sleddin' for her sometimes to get clo'es and grub for the famerly, without follerin' Bob around."

"Sharp girls, too, I reckon; one of them writes things for the magazines, does n't she? — Cynthia, eh?" said Mr. Hamlin, carelessly.

Evidently this fact was not a notorious one to the barkeeper. He, however, said, "Dunno; mabbee; her father was eddicated, and the widder Delatour, too, though she 's sorter queer, I 've heard tell.   Lord! Mr. Hamlin, *you* oughter remember old man Delatour! From Opelousas, Louisiany, you know! High old sport — French style, frilled bosom — open-handed, and us'ter buck ag'in' faro awful!   Why, he dropped a heap o' money to *you* over in San José two years ago at poker!   You must remember him!"

The slightest possible flush passed over Mr. Hamlin's brow under the shadow of his hat, but did not get lower than his eyes. He suddenly *had* recalled the spendthrift Delatour perfectly, and as quickly regretted now that he had not doubled the honorarium he had just sent to his portionless daughter. But he only said, coolly, "No," and then, raising his pale face and audacious eyes, continued in his laziest and most insulting manner, "no: the fact is, my mind is just now preoccupied in wondering if the gas is leaking anywhere, and if anything is ever served over this bar except elegant conversation.   When the gentleman who mixes drinks comes back, perhaps you 'll be good enough to tell him to send a whisky sour to Mr. Jack Hamlin in the parlor.   Meantime, you can turn off your soda fountain: I don't want any fizz in mine."

Having thus quite recovered himself, Mr. Hamlin lounged gracefully across the hall into the parlor. As he did so, a darkish young man, with a slim boyish figure, a thin face, and a discontented expression, rose from an armchair, held out his hand, and, with a saturnine smile, said : —

"Jack !"

"Fred !"

The two men remained gazing at each other with a half-amused, half-guarded expression. Mr. Hamlin was first to begin. "I did n't think *you 'd* be such a fool as to try on this kind of thing, Fred," he said, half seriously.

"Yes, but it was to keep you from being a much bigger one that I hunted you up," said the editor, mischievously. "Read that. I got it an hour after you left." And he placed a little triumphantly in Jack's hand the letter he had received from White Violet.

Mr. Hamlin read it with an unmoved face, and then laid his two hands on the editor's shoulders. "Yes, my young friend, and you sat down and wrote her a pretty letter and sent her twenty dollars — which, permit me to say, was d—d poor pay ! But that is n't

your fault, I reckon : it's the meanness of
your proprietors."

"But it isn't the question, either, just
now, Jack, however you have been able to
answer it. Do you mean to say seriously
that you want to know anything more of a
woman who could write such a letter ? "

"I don't know," said Jack, cheerfully.
"She might be a devilish sight funnier than
if she had n't written it — which is the fact."

"You mean to say *she* did n't write it ? "

"Yes."

"Who did, then ? "

"Her brother Bob."

After a moment's scrutiny of his friend's
bewildered face, Mr. Hamlin briefly related
his adventures, from the moment of his meeting Bob at the mountain-stream to the barkeeper's gossiping comment and sequel.
"Therefore," he concluded, "the author of
'Underbrush' is Miss Cynthia Delatour, one
of four daughters of a widow who lives two
miles from here at the crossing. I shall see
her this evening and make sure ; but to-
morrow morning you will pay me the breakfast you owe me. She's good-looking, but
I can't say I fancy the poetic style : it's a
little too high-toned for me. However, I

love my love with a C, because she is your
Contributor; I hate her with a C, because
of her Connections; I met her by Chance
and treated her with Civility; her name is
Cynthia, and she lives on a Cross-road."

"But you surely don't expect you will
ever see Bob, again!" said the editor, impatiently. "You have trusted him with enough
to start him for the Sandwich Islands, to
say nothing of the ruinous precedent you
have established in his mind of the value of
poetry. I am surprised that a man of your
knowledge of the world would have faith in
that imp the second time."

"My knowledge of the world," returned
Mr. Hamlin, sententiously, "tells me that's
the only way you can trust anybody. *Once*
doesn't make a habit, nor show a character.
I could see by his bungling that he had never
tried this on before. Just now the temptation to wipe out his punishment by doing the
square thing, and coming back a sort of hero,
is stronger than any other. 'T is n't everybody that gets that chance," he added, with
an odd laugh.

Nevertheless, three hours passed without
bringing Bob. The two men had gone to
the billiard-room, when a waiter brought a

note, which he handed to Mr. Hamlin with some apologetic hesitation. It bore no super-scription, but had been brought by a boy who described Mr. Hamlin perfectly, and requested that the note should be handed to him with the remark that " Bob had come back."

" And is he there now ? " asked Mr. Ham-lin, holding the letter unopened in his hand.

" No, sir ; he run right off."

The editor laughed, but Mr. Hamlin, hav-ing perused the note, put away his cue. " Come into my room," he said.

The editor followed, and Mr. Hamlin laid the note before him on the table. " Bob 's all right," he said, " for I 'll bet a thousand dollars that note is genuine."

It was delicately written, in a cultivated feminine hand, utterly unlike the scrawl that had first excited the editor's curiosity, and ran as follows : —

He who brought me the bounty of your friend — for I cannot call a recompense so far above my deserts by any other name — gives me also to understand that you wished for an interview. I cannot believe that this is mere idle curiosity, or that you have any

motive that is not kindly and honorable, but
I feel that I must beg and pray you not to
seek to remove the veil behind which I have
chosen to hide myself and my poor efforts
from identification. I *think* I know you —
I *know* I know myself — well enough to believe it would give neither of us any happi-
ness. You will say to your generous friend
that he has already given the Unknown more
comfort and hope than could come from any
personal compliment or publicity, and you
will yourself believe that you have all un-
consciously brightened a sad woman's fancy
with a Dream and a Vision that before to-
day had been unknown to

WHITE VIOLET.

"Have you read it?" asked Mr. Hamlin.
"Yes."

"Then you don't want to see it any more,
or even remember you ever saw it," said Mr.
Hamlin, carefully tearing the note into small
pieces and letting them drift from the windows like blown blossoms.

"But, I say, Jack! look here; I don't understand! You say you have already seen
this woman, and yet" —

"I *have n't* seen her," said Jack, composedly, turning from the window.

" What do you mean? "

" I mean that you and I, Fred, are going to drop this fooling right here and leave this place for Frisco by first stage to-morrow, and — that I owe you that dinner."

WHEN the stage for San Francisco rolled away the next morning with Mr. Hamlin and the editor, the latter might have recognized in the occupant of a dust-covered buggy that was coming leisurely towards them the tall figure, long beard, and straight duster of his late visitor, Mr. James Bowers. For Mr. Bowers was on the same quest that the others had just abandoned. Like Mr. Hamlin, he had been left to his own resources, but Mr. Bowers's resources were a life-long experience and technical skill; he too had noted the topographical indications of the poem, and his knowledge of the sylva of Upper California pointed as unerringly as Mr. Hamlin's luck to the cryptogamous haunts of the Summit. Such abnormal growths were indicative of certain localities only, but, as they were not remunerative from a pecuniary point of view, were to be avoided by the sagacious woodman. It was clear, therefore, that Mr. Bowers's visit to

Green Springs was not professional, and that he did not even figuratively accept the omen.

He baited and rested his horse at the hotel, where his bucolic exterior, however, did not elicit that attention which had been accorded to Mr. Hamlin's charming insolence or the editor's cultivated manner. But he glanced over a township map on the walls of the reading-room, and took note of the names of the owners of different lots, farms, and ranches, passing that of Delatour with the others. Then he drove leisurely in the direction of the woods, and, reaching them, tied his horse to a young sapling in the shade, and entered their domain with a shambling but familiar woodman's step.

It is not the purpose of this brief chronicle to follow Mr. Bowers in his professional diagnosis of the locality. He recognized Nature in one of her moods of wasteful extravagance, — a waste that his experienced eye could tell was also sapping the vitality of those outwardly robust shafts that rose around him. He knew, without testing them, that half of these fair-seeming columns were hollow and rotten at the core; he could detect the chill odor of decay through the hot balsamic spices stirred by the wind that streamed through their long aisles, — like incense mingling with the exhalations of a crypt. He stopped now and then to part the heavy fronds down to their roots in the dank moss, seeing again, as he had told the editor, the weird *second* twilight through their miniature stems, and the microcosm of life that filled it. But, even while paying this tribute to the accuracy of the unknown poetess, he was, like his predecessor, haunted more strongly by the atmosphere and melody of her verse. Its spell was upon him, too. Unlike Mr. Hamlin, he did not sing. He only halted once or twice, silently combing his straight narrow beard with his three fingers, until the action seemed to draw down the lines of his face into limitless dejection, and an inscrutable melancholy filled his small gray eyes. The few birds which had hailed Mr. Hamlin as their successful rival fled away before the grotesque and angular half-length of Mr. Bowers, as if the wind had blown in a scarecrow from the distant farms.

Suddenly he observed the figure of a woman, with her back towards him, leaning motionless against a tree, and apparently

gazing intently in the direction of Green
Springs. He had approached so near to her
that it was singular she had not heard him.
Mr. Bowers was a bashful man in the presence of the other sex. He felt exceedingly
embarrassed; if he could have gone away
without attracting her attention he would
have done so. Neither could he remain silent, a tacit spy of her meditation. He had
recourse to a polite but singularly artificial
cough.

To his surprise, she gave a faint cry,
turned quickly towards him, and then shrank
back and lapsed quite helpless against the
tree. Her evident distress overcame his
bashfulness. He ran towards her.

"I'm sorry I frighted ye, ma'am, but I
was afraid I might skeer ye more if I lay
low, and said nothin'."

Even then, if she had been some fair
young country girl, he would have relapsed
after this speech into his former bashfulness.
But the face and figure she turned towards
him were neither young nor fair: a woman
past forty, with gray threads and splashes
in her brushed-back hair, which was turned
over her ears in two curls like frayed strands
of rope. Her forehead was rather high than

broad, her nose large but well-shaped, and her eyes full but so singularly light in color as to seem almost sightless. The short upper lip of her large mouth displayed her teeth in an habitual smile, which was in turn so flatly contradicted by every other line of her careworn face that it seemed gratuitously artificial. Her figure was hidden by a shapeless garment that partook equally of the shawl, cloak, and wrapper.

"I am very foolish," she began, in a voice and accent that at once asserted a cultivated woman, "but I so seldom meet anybody here that a voice quite startled me. That, and the heat," she went on, wiping her face, into which the color was returning violently — "for I seldom go out as early as this — I suppose affected me."

Mr. Bowers had that innate Far-Western reverence for womanhood which I fancy challenges the most polished politeness. He remained patient, undemonstrative, self-effacing, and respectful before her, his angular arm slightly but not obtrusively advanced, the offer of protection being in the act rather than in any spoken word, and requiring no response.

"Like as not, ma'am," he said, cheerfully,

looking everywhere but in her burning face.
" The sun *is* pow'ful hot at this time o' day;
I felt it myself comin' yer, and, though the
damp of this timber kinder sets it back, it's
likely to come out ag'in. Ye can't check it
no more than the sap in that choked limb
thar " — he pointed ostentatiously where a
fallen pine had been caught in the bent and
twisted arm of another, but which still put
out a few green tassels beyond the point of
impact. " Do you live far from here,
ma'am ? " he added.

" Only as far as the first turning below
the hill."

" I 've got my buggy here, and I 'm goin'
that way, and I can jist set ye down thar
cool and comfortable. Ef," he continued,
in the same assuring tone, without waiting
for a reply, " ye 'll jist take a good grip of
my arm thar," curving his wrist and hand
behind him like a shepherd's crook, " I 'll
go first, and break away the brush for ye."

She obeyed mechanically, and they fared
on through the thick ferns in this fashion
for some moments, he looking ahead, occasionally dropping a word of caution or en-
couragement, but never glancing at her face.
When they reached the buggy he lifted her

into it carefully, — and perpendicularly, it struck her afterwards, very much as if she had been a transplanted sapling with bared and sensitive roots, — and then gravely took his place beside her.

"Bein' in the timber trade myself, ma'am," he said, gathering up the reins, "I chanced to sight these woods, and took a look around. My name is Bowers, of Mendocino; I reckon there ain't much that grows in the way o' standin' timber on the Pacific Slope that I don't know and can't locate, though I *do* say it. I 've got ez big a mill, and ez big a run in my district, ez there is anywhere. Ef you 're ever up my way, you ask for Bowers — Jim Bowers — and that 's *me*."

There is probably nothing more conducive to conversation between strangers than a wholesome and early recognition of each other's foibles. Mr. Bowers, believing his chance acquaintance a superior woman, naïvely spoke of himself in a way that he hoped would reassure her that she was not compromising herself in accepting his civility, and so satisfy what must be her inevitable pride. On the other hand, the woman regained her self-possession by this exhibition of Mr. Bowers's vanity, and, revived by the refreshing breeze caused by the rapid motion of the buggy along the road, thanked him graciously.

"I suppose there are many strangers at the Green Springs Hotel," she said, after a pause.

"I did n't get to see 'em, as I only put up my hoss there," he replied. "But I know the stage took some away this mornin': it seemed pretty well loaded up when I passed it."

The woman drew a deep sigh. The act struck Mr. Bowers as a possible return of her former nervous weakness. Her attention must at once be distracted at any cost — even conversation.

"Perhaps," he began, with sudden and appalling lightness, "I 'm a-talkin' to Mrs. McFadden?"

"No," said the woman, abstractedly.

"Then it must be Mrs. Delatour? There are only two township lots on that cross-road."

"My name *is* Delatour," she said, somewhat wearily.

Mr. Bowers was conversationally stranded. He was not at all anxious to know her name, yet, knowing it now, it seemed to suggest that there was nothing more to say. He would, of course, have preferred to ask her if she had read the poetry about the Underbrush, and if she knew the poetess, and what she thought of it ; but the fact that she appeared to be an " eddicated " woman made him sensitive of displaying technical ignorance in his manner of talking about it. She might ask him if it was " subjective " or " objective " — two words he had heard used at the Debating Society at Mendocino on the question, " Is poetry morally beneficial? " For a few moments he was silent. But presently she took the initiative in conversation, at first slowly and abstractedly, and then, as if appreciating his sympathetic reticence, or mayhap finding some relief in monotonous expression, talked mechanically, deliberately, but unostentatiously about herself. So colorless was her intonation that at times it did not seem as if she was talking to him, but repeating some conversation she had held with another.

She had lived there ever since she had been in California. Her husband had bought the Spanish title to the property when they first married. The property at his death was found to be greatly involved ;

she had been obliged to part with much of it to support her children — four girls and a boy. She had been compelled to withdraw the girls from the convent at Santa Clara to help about the house; the boy was too young — she feared, too shiftless — to do anything. The farm did not pay; the land was poor; she knew nothing about farming; she had been brought up in New Orleans, where her father had been a judge, and she did n't understand country life. Of course she had been married too young — as all girls were. Lately she had thought of selling off and moving to San Francisco, where she would open a boarding-house or a school for young ladies. He could advise her, perhaps, of some good opportunity. Her own girls were far enough advanced to assist her in teaching; one particularly, Cynthia, was quite clever, and spoke French and Spanish fluently.

As Mr. Bowers was familiar with many of these counts in the feminine American indictment of life generally, he was not perhaps greatly moved. But in the last sentence he thought he saw an opening to return to his main object, and, looking up cautiously, said : —

" And mebbe write po'try now and then ? "

To his great discomfiture, the only effect of this suggestion was to check his companion's. speech for some moments and apparently throw her back into her former abstraction. Yet, after a long pause, as they were turning into the lane, she said, as if continuing the subject : —

" I only hope that, whatever my daughters may do, they won't marry young."

The yawning breaches in the Delatour gates and fences presently came in view. They were supposed to be reinforced by half a dozen dogs, who, however, did their duty with what would seem to be the prevailing inefficiency, retiring after a single perfunctory yelp to shameless stretching, scratching, and slumber. Their places were taken on the veranda by two negro servants, two girls respectively of eight and eleven, and a boy of fourteen, who remained silently staring. As Mr. Bowers had accepted the widow's polite invitation to enter, she was compelled, albeit in an equally dazed and helpless way, to issue some preliminary orders : —

" Now, Chloe — I mean aunt Dinah — do take Eunice — I mean Victorine and

Una — away, and — you know — tidy them ;
and you, Sarah — it's Sarah, is n't it ? —
lay some refreshment in the parlor for this
gentleman.   And, Bob, tell your sister Cynthia to come here with Eunice."   As Bob
still remained staring at Mr. Bowers, she
added, in weary explanation, " Mr. Bowers
brought me over from the Summit woods in
his buggy — it was so hot.   There — shake
hands and thank him, and run away — do ! "

They crossed a broad but scantily - furnished hall.   Everywhere the same look of
hopeless incompleteness, temporary utility,
and premature decay ; most of the furniture
was mismatched and misplaced ; many of the
rooms had changed their original functions
or doubled them ; a smell of cooking came
from the library, on whose shelves, mingled
with books, were dresses and household
linen, and through the door of a room into
which Mrs. Delatour retired to remove her
duster Mr. Bowers caught a glimpse of a bed,
and of a table covered with books and papers, at which a tall, fair girl was writing.
In a few moments Mrs. Delatour returned,
accompanied by this girl, and Eunice, her
short-lipped sister.   Bob, who joined the
party seated around Mr. Bowers and a table

set with cake, a decanter, and glasses, completed the group. Emboldened by the presence of the tall Cynthia and his glimpse of her previous literary attitude, Mr. Bowers resolved to make one more attempt.

"I suppose these yer young ladies sometimes go to the wood, too?" As his eye rested on Cynthia, she replied: —

"Oh, yes."

"I reckon on account of the purty shadows down in the brush, and the soft light, eh? and all that?" he continued, with a playful manner but a serious accession of color.

"Why, the woods belong to us. It 's mar's property!" broke in Eunice with a flash of teeth.

"Well, Lordy, I wanter know!" said Mr. Bowers, in some astonishment. "Why, that 's right in my line, too! I 've been sightin' timber all along here, and that 's how I dropped in on yer mar." Then, seeing a look of eagerness light up the faces of Bob and Eunice, he was encouraged to make the most of his opportunity. "Why, ma'am," he went on, cheerfully, "I reckon you 're holdin' that wood at a pretty stiff figger, now."

"Why?" asked Mrs. Delatour, simply.

Mr. Bowers delivered a wink at Bob and Eunice, who were still watching him with anxiety. "Well, not on account of the actool timber, for the best of it ain't sound," he said, "but on account of its bein' famous! Everybody that reads that pow'ful pretty poem about it in the 'Excelsior Magazine' wants to see it. Why, it would pay the Green Springs hotel-keeper to buy it up for his customers. But I s'pose you reckon to keep it — along with the poetess — in your famerly?"

Although Mr. Bowers long considered this speech as the happiest and most brilliant effort of his life, its immediate effect was not, perhaps, all that could be desired. The widow turned upon him a restrained and darkening face. Cynthia half rose with an appealing "Oh, mar!" and Bob and Eunice, having apparently pinched each other to the last stage of endurance, retired precipitately from the room in a prolonged giggle.

"I have not yet thought of disposing of the Summit woods, Mr. Bowers," said Mrs. Delatour, coldly, "but if I should do so, I will consult you. You must excuse the children, who see so little company, they are quite unmanageable when strangers are present. Cynthia, *will* you see if the servants have looked after Mr. Bowers's horse? You know Bob is not to be trusted."

There was clearly nothing else for Mr. Bowers to do but to take his leave, which he did respectfully, if not altogether hopefully. But when he had reached the lane, his horse shied from the unwonted spectacle of Bob, swinging his hat, and apparently awaiting him, from the fork of a wayside sapling.

"Hol' up, mister. Look here!"

Mr. Bowers pulled up. Bob dropped into the road, and, after a backward glance over his shoulder, said : —

"Drive 'longside the fence in the shadder." As Mr. Bowers obeyed, Bob approached the wheels of the buggy in a manner half shy, half mysterious. "You wanter buy them Summit woods, mister?"

"Well, per'aps, sonny. Why?" smiled Mr. Bowers.

"Coz I'll tell ye suthin'. Don't you be fooled into allowin' that Cynthia wrote that po'try. She did n't — no more 'n Eunice nor me. Mar kinder let ye think it, 'cos she don't want folks to think *she* did it. But mar wrote that po'try herself; wrote it out

o' them thar woods — all by herself. Thar's
a heap more po'try thar, you bet, and jist as
good. And she's the one that kin write
it — you hear me? That's my mar, every
time! You buy that thar wood, and get
mar to run it for po'try, and you'll make
your pile, sure! I ain't lyin'. You'd better look spry : thar's another feller snoopin'
'round yere — only he barked up the wrong
tree, and thought it was Cynthia, jist as you
did."

"Another feller?" repeated the astonished
Bowers.

"Yes; a rig'lar sport. He was orful keen
on that po'try, too, you bet. So you'd better hump yourself afore somebody else cuts
in. Mar got a hundred dollars for that
pome, from that editor feller and his pard-
ner. I reckon that's the rig'lar price, eh?"
he added, with a sudden suspicious caution.

"I reckon so," replied Mr. Bowers,
blankly. "But — look here, Bob! Do you
mean to say it was your mother — your
mother, Bob, who wrote that poem? Are
you sure?"

"D' ye think I'm lyin'?" said Bob, scornfully. "Don't *I* know? Don't I copy 'em
out plain for her, so as folks won't know

her handwrite? Go 'way! you 're loony!"
Then, possibly doubting if this latter expression were strictly diplomatic with the
business in hand, he added, in half-reproach,
half-apology, " Don't ye see I don't want ye
to be fooled into losin' yer chance o' buying
up that Summit wood? It 's the cold truth
I 'm tellin' ye."

Mr. Bowers no longer doubted it. Disappointed as he undoubtedly was at first, —
and even self-deceived, — he recognized in a
flash the grim fact that the boy had stated.
He recalled the apparition of the sad-faced
woman in the wood — her distressed manner,
that to his inexperienced mind now took
upon itself the agitated trembling of disturbed mystic inspiration. A sense of sadness and remorse succeeded his first shock
of disappointment.

" Well, are ye going to buy the woods?"
said Bob, eying him grimly. " Ye 'd better
say."

Mr. Bowers started. " I should n't wonder, Bob," he said, with a smile, gathering
up his reins. " Anyhow, I 'm comin' back
to see your mother this afternoon. And
meantime, Bob, you keep the first chance for
me."

He drove away, leaving the youthful diplo-
matist standing with his bare feet in the dust.
For a minute or two the young gentleman
amused himself by a few light saltatory steps
in the road.   Then a smile of scornful superiority, mingled perhaps with a sense of previous slights and unappreciation, drew back
his little upper lip, and brightened his mot-
tled cheek.

"I 'd like ter know," he said, darkly,
"what this yer God-forsaken famerly would
do without *me!*"

CHAPTER V.

It is to be presumed that the editor and Mr. Hamlin mutually kept to their tacit agreement to respect the impersonality of the poetess, for during the next three months the subject was seldom alluded to by either. Yet in that period White Violet had sent two other contributions, and on each occasion Mr. Hamlin had insisted upon increasing the honorarium to the amount of his former gift. In vain the editor pointed out the danger of this form of munificence; Mr. Hamlin retorted by saying that if he refused he would appeal to the proprietor, who certainly would not object to taking the credit of this liberality. "As to the risks," concluded Jack, sententiously, "I'll take them; and as far as you're concerned, you certainly get the worth of your money."

Indeed, if popularity was an indiction, this had become suddenly true. For the poetess's third contribution, without changing its strong local color and individuality, had

been an unexpected outburst of human passion — a love-song, that touched those to
whom the subtler meditative graces of the
poetess had been unknown. Many people
had listened to this impassioned but despairing cry from some remote and charmed solitude, who had never read poetry before, who
translated it into their own limited vocab-
ulary and more limited experience, and were
inexpressibly affected to find that they, too,
understood it ; it was caught up and echoed
by the feverish, adventurous, and unsatisfied
life that filled that day and time.   Even the
editor was surprised and frightened.   Like
most cultivated men, he distrusted popularity; like all men who believe in their own
individual judgment, he doubted collective
wisdom.   Yet now that his *protégée* had been
accepted by others, he questioned that judgment and became her critic.   It struck him
that her sudden outburst was strained ; it
seemed to him that in this mere contortion
of passion the sibyl's robe had become rudely
disarranged.   He spoke to Hamlin, and even
approached the tabooed subject.

"Did you see anything that suggested this
sort of business in — in — that woman — I
mean in — your pilgrimage, Jack ?"

" No," responded Jack, gravely. " But it's easy to see she's got hold of some hay-footed fellow up there in the mountains with straws in his hair, and is playing him for all he's worth. You won't get much more poetry out of her, I reckon."

Is was not long after this conversation that one afternoon, when the editor was alone, Mr. James Bowers entered the editorial room with much of the hesitation and irresolution of his previous visit. As the editor had not only forgotten him, but even dissociated him with the poetess, Mr. Bowers was fain to meet his unresponsive eye and manner with some explanation.

" Ye disremember my comin' here, Mr. Editor, to ask you the name o' the lady who called herself ' White Violet,' and how you allowed you couldn't give it, but would write and ask for it ? "

Mr. Editor, leaning back in his chair, now remembered the occurrence, but was distressed to add that the situation remained unchanged, and that he had received no such permission.

" Never mind *that*, my lad," said Mr. Bowers, gravely, waving his hand. " I understand all that ; but, ez I've known the lady ever since, and am now visiting her at her house on the Summit, I reckon it don't make much matter."

It was quite characteristic of Mr. Bowers's smileless earnestness that he made no ostentation of this dramatic retort, nor of the undisguised stupefaction of the editor.

" Do you mean to say that you have met White Violet, the author of these poems?" repeated the editor.

" Which her name is Delatour, — the widder Delatour, — ez she has herself give me permission to tell you," continued Mr. Bowers, with a certain abstracted and automatic precision that dissipated any suggestion of malice in the reversed situation.

" Delatour! — a widow!" repeated the editor.

" With five children," continued Mr. Bowers. Then, with unalterable gravity, he briefly gave an outline of her condition and the circumstances of his acquaintance with her.

" But I reckoned *you* might have known suthin' o' this; though she never let on you did," he concluded, eying the editor with troubled curiosity.

The editor did not think it necessary to

implicate Mr. Hamlin. He said, briefly, "I? Oh, no!"

"Of course, *you* might not have seen her?" said Mr. Bowers, keeping the same grave, troubled gaze on the editor.

"Of course not," said the editor, somewhat impatient under the singular scrutiny of Mr. Bowers; "and I'm very anxious to know how she looks. Tell me, what is she like?"

"She is a fine, pow'ful, eddicated woman," said Mr. Bowers, with slow deliberation. "Yes, sir, — a pow'ful woman, havin' grand ideas of her own, and holdin' to 'em." He had withdrawn his eyes from the editor, and apparently addressed the ceiling in confidence.

"But what does she look like, Mr. Bowers?" said the editor, smiling.

"Well, sir, she looks — *like* — *it!* Yes," — with deliberate caution, — "I should say, just like it."

After a pause, apparently to allow the editor to materialize this ravishing description, he said, gently, "Are you busy just now?"

"Not very. What can I do for you?"

"Well, not much for *me*, I reckon," he

returned, with a deeper respiration, that was his nearest approach to a sigh, " but suthin' perhaps for yourself and — another. Are you married ? "

" No," said the editor, promptly.

" Nor engaged to any — young lady ? " — with great politeness.

" No."

" Well, mebbe you think it a queer thing for me to say, — mebbe you reckon you *know* it ez well ez anybody, — but it 's my opinion that White Violet is in love with you."

" With me ? " ejaculated the editor, in a hopeless astonishment that at last gave way to an incredulous and irresistible laugh.

A slight touch of pain passed over Mr. Bowers's dejected face, but left the deep outlines set with a rude dignity. " It 's *so*," he said, slowly, " though, as a young man and a gay feller, ye may think it 's funny."

" No, not funny, but a terrible blunder, Mr. Bowers, for I give you my word I know nothing of the lady and have never set eyes upon her."

" No, but she has on *you*. I can't say," continued Mr. Bowers, with sublime *naïveté*, " that I 'd ever recognize you from her description, but a woman o' that kind don't see with her eyes like you and me, but with all her senses to onct, and a heap more that ain't senses as we know 'em. The same· eyes that seed down through the brush and ferns in the Summit woods, the same ears that heerd the music of the wind trailin' through the pines, don't see you with my eyes or hear you with my ears. And when she paints you, it's nat'ril for a woman with that pow'ful mind and grand idees to dip her brush into her heart's blood for warmth and color. Yer smilin', young man. Well, go on and smile at me, my lad, but not at her. For you don't know her. When you know her story as I do, when you know she was made a wife afore she ever knew what it was to be a young woman, when you know that the man she married never understood the kind o' critter he was tied to no more than ef he'd been a steer yoked to a Morgan colt, when ye know she had children growin' up around her afore she had given over bein' a sort of child herself, when ye know she worked and slaved for that man and those children about the house — her heart, her soul, and all her pow'ful mind bein' all the time in the woods along with the flickerin'

leaves and the shadders, — when ye mind
she could n't get the small ways o' the ranch
because she had the big ways o' Natur' that
made it, — then you 'll understand her."

Impressed by the sincerity of his visitor's
manner, touched by the unexpected poetry
of his appeal, and yet keenly alive to the
absurdity of an incomprehensible blunder
somewhere committed, the editor gasped almost hysterically, —

" But why should all this make her in
love with *me?* "

" Because ye are both gifted," returned
Mr. Bowers, with sad but unconquerable
conviction; " because ye 're both, so to speak,
in a line o' idees and business that draws ye
together, — to lean on each other and trust
each other ez pardners. Not that *ye* are
ezakly her ekal," he went on, with a return
to his previous exasperating *naïveté*, " though
I 've heerd promisin' things of ye, and ye 're
still young, but in matters o' this kind there
is allers one ez hez to be looked up to by the
other, — and gin'rally the wrong one. She
looks up to you, Mr. Editor, — it 's part of her
po'try, — ez she looks down inter the brush
and sees more than is plain to you and me.
Not," he continued, with a courteously depre-

cating wave of the hand, " ez you hain't bin
kind to her — mebbe *too* kind. For thar 's
the purty letter you writ her, thar 's the per-
lite, easy, captivatin' way you had with her
gals and that boy — hold on ! " — as the
editor made a gesture of despairing renunci-
ation, — " I ain't sayin' you ain't right in
keepin' it to yourself, — and thar 's the extry money you sent her every time. Stop!
she knows it was *extry*, for she made a p'int
o' gettin' me to find out the market price o'
po'try in papers and magazines, and she
reckons you 've bin payin' her four hundred
per cent. above them figgers — hold on! I
ain't sayin' it ain't free and liberal in you,
and I 'd have done the same thing ; yet *she*
thinks " —

But the editor had risen hastily to his feet
with flushing cheeks.

" One moment, Mr. Bowers," he said,
hurriedly. " This is the most dreadful
blunder of all. The gift is not mine. It
was the spontaneous offering of another who
really admired our friend's work, — a gentleman who " — He stopped suddenly.

The sound of a familiar voice, lightly
humming, was borne along the passage ; the
light tread of a familiar foot was approach-

ing. The editor turned quickly towards the
open door, — so quickly that Mr. Bowers
was fain to turn also.

For a charming instant the figure of Jack
Hamlin, handsome, careless, and confident,
was framed in the doorway. His dark eyes,
with their habitual scorn of his average
fellow-man, swept superciliously over Mr.
Bowers, and rested for an instant with caressing familiarity on the editor.

" Well, sonny, any news from the old girl
at the Summit ? "

"No-o," hastily stammered the editor,
with a half-hysterical laugh. " No, Jack.
Excuse me a moment."

" All right ; busy, I see. *Hasta mañana.*"

The picture vanished, the frame was
empty.

" You see," continued the editor, turning
to Mr. Bowers, " there has been a mistake.
I " — but he stopped suddenly at the ashen
face of Mr. Bowers, still fixed in the direction of the vanished figure.

" Are you ill ? "

Mr. Bowers did not reply, but slowly withdrew his eyes, and turned them heavily on
the editor. Then, drawing a longer, deeper
breath, he picked up his soft felt hat, and,

moulding it into shape in his hands as if preparing to put it on, he moistened his dry, grayish lips, and said, gently : —

" Friend o' yours ? "

" Yes," said the editor — " Jack Hamlin. Of course, you know him ? "

" Yes."

Mr. Bowers here put his hat on his head, and, after a pause, turned round slowly once or twice, as if he had forgotten it, and was still seeking it. Finally he succeeded in finding the editor's hand, and shook it, albeit his own trembled slightly. Then he said : —

" I reckon you 're right. There 's bin a mistake. I see it now. Good-by. If you 're ever up my way, drop in and see me." He then walked to the doorway, passed out, and seemed to melt into the afternoon shadows of the hall.

He never again entered the office of the " Excelsior Magazine," neither was any further contribution ever received from White Violet. To a polite entreaty from the editor, addressed first to " White Violet " and then to Mrs. Delatour, there was no response. The thought of Mr. Hamlin's cynical prophecy disturbed him, but that gentleman, preoccupied in filling some professional

engagements in Sacramento, gave him no
chance to acquire further explanations as to
the past or the future.   The youthful editor
was at first in despair and filled with a vague
remorse of some unfulfilled duty.   But, to
his surprise, the readers of the magazine
seemed to survive their talented contributor,
and the feverish life that had been thrilled
by her song, in two months had apparently
forgotten her.   Nor was her voice lifted
from any alien quarter; the domestic and foreign press that had echoed her lays seemed
to respond no longer to her utterance.

It is possible that some readers of these
pages may remember a previous chronicle
by the same historian wherein it was recorded
that the volatile spirit of Mr. Hamlin,
slightly assisted by circumstances, passed
beyond these voices at the Ranch of the
Blessed Fisherman, some two years later.
As the editor stood beside the body of his
friend on the morning of the funeral, he
noticed among the flowers laid upon his bier
by loving hands a wreath of white violets.
Touched and disturbed by a memory long
since forgotten, he was further embarrassed,
as the *cortège* dispersed in the Mission grave-
yard, by the apparition of the tall figure of

Mr. James Bowers from behind a monumental column. The editor turned to him quickly.

"I am glad to see you here," he said, awkwardly, and he knew not why; then, after a pause, "I trust you can give me some news of Mrs. Delatour. I wrote to her nearly two years ago, but had no response."

"Thar's bin no Mrs. Delatour for two years," said Mr. Bowers, contemplatively stroking his beard; "and mebbe that's why. She's bin for two years Mrs. Bowers."

"I congratulate you," said the editor; "but I hope there still remains a White Violet, and that, for the sake of literature, she has not given up" —

"Mrs. Bowers," interrupted Mr. Bowers, with singular deliberation, "found that makin' po'try and tendin' to the cares of a growin'-up famerly was irritatin' to the narves. They did n't jibe, so to speak. What Mrs. Bowers wanted — and what, po'try or no po'try, I 've bin tryin' to give her — was Rest! She's bin havin' it comfor'bly up at my ranch at Mendocino, with her children and me. Yes, sir" — his eye wandered accidentally to the new-made grave — "you 'll excuse my sayin' it to a man in your profession, but it 's what most folks will find is a heap better than readin' or writin' or actin' po'try — and that 's — Rest! "

THE CHATELAINE OF BURNT RIDGE.

CHAPTER I.

It had grown dark on Burnt Ridge. Seen from below, the whole serrated crest that had glittered in the sunset as if its interstices were eaten by consuming fires, now closed up its ranks of blackened shafts and became again harsh and sombre *chevaux de frise* against the sky. A faint glow still lingered over the red valley road, as if it were its own reflection, rather than any light from beyond the darkened ridge. Night was already creeping up out of remote cañons and along the furrowed flanks of the mountain, or settling on the nearer woods with the sound of home-coming and innumerable wings. At a point where the road began to encroach upon the mountainside in its slow winding ascent the darkness had become so real that a young girl cantering along the rising terrace found difficulty in guiding her horse, with eyes still dazzled by the sunset fires.

In spite of her precautions, the animal suddenly shied at some object in the obscured roadway, and nearly unseated her. The accident disclosed not only the fact that she was riding in a man's saddle, but also a foot and ankle that her ordinary walking-dress was too short to hide. It was evident that her equestrian exercise was extempore, and that at that hour and on that road she had not expected to meet company. But she was apparently a good horsewoman, for the mischance which might have thrown a less practical or more timid rider seemed of little moment to her. With a strong hand and determined gesture she wheeled her frightened horse back into the track, and rode him directly at the object. But here she herself slightly recoiled, for it was the body of a man lying in the road.

As she leaned forward over her horse's shoulder, she could see by the dim light that he was a miner, and that, though motionless, he was breathing stertorously. Drunk, no doubt! — an accident of the locality alarming only to her horse. But although she cantered impatiently forward, she had not proceeded a hundred yards before she stopped reflectively, and trotted back again. He had not moved. She could now see that his head and shoulders were covered with broken clods of earth and gravel, and smaller fragments lay at his side. A dozen feet above him on the hillside there was a foot trail which ran parallel with the bridle-road, and occasionally overhung it. It seemed possible that he might have fallen from the trail and been stunned.

Dismounting, she succeeded in dragging him to a safer position by the bank. The act discovered his face, which was young, and unknown to her. Wiping it with the silk handkerchief which was loosely slung around his neck after the fashion of his class, she gave a quick feminine glance around her and then approached her own and rather handsome face near his lips. There was no odor of alcohol in the thick and heavy res-piration. Mounting again, she rode forward at an accelerated pace, and in twenty minutes had reached a higher tableland of the mountain, a cleared opening in the forest that showed signs of careful cultivation, and a large, rambling, yet picturesque-looking dwelling, whose unpainted red-wood walls were hidden in roses and creepers. Pushing open a swinging gate, she entered the inclosure as a brown-faced man, dressed as a vaquero, came towards her as if to assist her to alight. But she had already leaped to the ground and thrown him the reins.

"Miguel," she said, with a mistress's quiet authority in her boyish contralto voice, "put Glory in the covered wagon, and drive down the road as far as the valley turning. There's a man lying near the right bank, drunk, or sick, may be, or perhaps crippled by a fall. Bring him up here, unless somebody has found him already, or you happen to know who he is and where to take him."

The vaquero raised his shoulders, half in disappointed expectation of some other command. "And your brother, señora, he has not himself arrived."

A light shadow of impatience crossed her face. "No," she said, bluntly. "Come, be quick."

She turned towards the house as the man moved away. Already a gaunt-looking old man had appeared in the porch, and was awaiting her with his hand shadowing his angry, suspicious eyes, and his lips moving querulously.

" Of course, you 've got to stand out there and give orders and 'tend to your own business afore you think o' speaking to your own flesh and blood," he said aggrievedly. " That 's all *you* care ! "

" There was a sick man lying in the road, and I 've sent Miguel to look after him," returned the girl, with a certain contemptuous resignation.

" Oh, yes!" struck in another voice, which seemed to belong to the female of the first speaker's species, and to be its equal in age and temper, " and I reckon you saw a jay bird on a tree, or a squirrel on the fence, and either of 'em was more important to you than your own brother."

"Steve did n't come by the stage, and did n't send any message," continued the young girl, with the same coldly resigned manner. "No one had any news of him, and, as I told you before, I did n't expect any."

" Why don't you say right out you did n't *want* any ? " said the old man, sneeringly. "Much you inquired ! No ; I orter hev gone myself, and I would if I was master here, instead of me and your mother bein' the dust of the yearth beneath your feet."

The young girl entered the house, followed by the old man, passing an old woman seated by the window, who seemed to be nursing her resentment and a large Bible which she held clasped against her shawled bosom at the same moment. Going to the wall, she hung up her large hat and slightly shook the red dust from her skirts as she continued her explanation, in the same deep voice, with a certain monotony of logic and possibly of purpose and practice also.

"You and mother know as well as I do, father, that Stephen is no more to be depended upon than the wind that blows. It's three years since he has been promising to come, and even getting money to come, and yet he has never showed his face, though he has been a dozen times within five miles of this house. He does n't come because he does n't want to come. As to *your* going over to the stage-office, I went there myself at the last moment to save you the mortification of asking questions of strangers that they know have been a dozen times answered already."

There was such a ring of absolute truthfulness, albeit worn by repetition, in the young girl's deep honest voice that for one instant her two more emotional relatives quailed before it; but only for a moment.

" That's right!" shrilled the old woman. " Go on and abuse your own brother. It's only the fear you have that he 'll make his fortune yet and shame you before the father and mother you despise."

The young girl remained standing by the window, motionless and apparently passive, as if receiving an accepted and usual punishment. But here the elder woman gave way to sobs and some incoherent snuffling, at which the younger went away. Whether she recognized in her mother's tears the ordinary deliquescence of emotion, or whether, as a woman herself, she knew that this mere feminine conventionality could not possibly be directed at her, and that the actual conflict between them had ceased, she passed slowly on to an inner hall, leaving the male victim, her unfortunate father, to succumb, as he always did sooner or later, to their influence. Crossing the hall, which was decorated with a few elk horns, Indian trophies, and mountain pelts, she entered another room, and closed the door behind her with a gesture of relief.

The room, which looked upon a porch,

presented a singular combination of masculine business occupations and feminine taste and adornment. A desk covered with papers, a shelf displaying a ledger and account-books, another containing works of reference, a table with a vase of flowers and a lady's riding-whip upon it, a map of California flanked on either side by an embroidered silken workbag and an oval mirror decked with grasses, a calendar and interest-table hanging below two school-girl crayons of classic heads with the legend, " Josephine Forsyth *fecit*," — were part of its incongruous accessories. The young girl went to her desk, but presently moved and turned towards the window thoughtfully. The last gleam had died from the steel-blue sky ; a few lights like star points began to prick out the lower valley. The expression of monotonous restraint and endurance had not yet faded from her face.

Yet she had been accustomed to scenes like the one she had just passed through since her girlhood. Five years ago, Alexander Forsyth, her uncle, had brought her to this spot — then a mere log cabin on the hillside — as a refuge from the impoverished and shiftless home of his elder brother

Thomas and his ill-tempered wife. Here
Alexander Forsyth, by reason of his more
dominant character and business capacity,
had prospered until he became a rich and
influential ranch owner. Notwithstanding
her father's jealousy of Alexander's fortune,
and the open rupture that followed between
the brothers, Josephine retained her position
in the heart and home of her uncle without
espousing the cause of either; and her father was too prudent not to recognize the
near and prospective advantages of such a
mediator. Accustomed to her parents' extravagant denunciations, and her uncle's
more repressed but practical contempt of
them, the unfortunate girl early developed
a cynical disbelief in the virtues of kinship
in the abstract, and a philosophical resignation to its effects upon her personally. Believing that her father and uncle fairly represented the fraternal principle, she was
quite prepared for the early defection and
distrust of her vagabond and dissipated
brother Stephen, and accepted it calmly.
True to an odd standard of justice, which
she had erected from the crumbling ruins of
her own domestic life, she was tolerant of
everything but human perfection. This

quality, however fatal to her higher growth, had given her a peculiar capacity for business which endeared her to her uncle. Familiar with the strong passions and prejudices of men, she had none of those feminine meannesses, a wholesome distrust of which had kept her uncle a bachelor. It was not strange, therefore, that when he died two years ago it was found that he had left her his entire property, real and personal, limited only by a single condition. She was to undertake the vocation of a " sole trader," and carry on the business under the name of " J. Forsyth." If she married, the estate and property was to be held distinct from her husband's, inalienable under the " Married Woman's Property Act," and subject during her life only to her own control and personal responsibilities as a trader.

The intense disgust and discomfiture of her parents, who had expected to more actively participate in their brother's fortune, may be imagined. But it was not equal to their fury when Josephine, instead of providing for them a separate maintenance out of her abundance, simply offered to transfer them and her brother to her own house on a domestic but not a business equality. There being no alternative but their former precarious shiftless life in their " played-out " claim in the valley, they wisely consented, reserving the sacred right of daily protest and objurgation. In the economy of Burnt Ridge Ranch they alone took it upon themselves to represent the shattered domestic altar and its outraged Lares and Penates. And so conscientiously did they perform their task as even occasionally to impede the business visitor to the ranch, and to cause some of the more practical neighbors seriously to doubt the young girl's commercial wisdom. But she was firm. Whether she thought her parents a necessity of respectable domesticity, or whether she regarded their presence in the light of a penitential atonement for some previous disregard of them, no one knew. Public opinion inclined to the latter.

The black line of ridge faded out with her abstraction, and she turned from the window and lit the lamp on her desk. The yellow light illuminated her face and figure. In their womanly graces there was no trace of what some people believed to be a masculine character, except a singularly frank look of critical inquiry and patient attention in her dark eyes. Her long brown hair was somewhat rigidly twisted into a knot on the top of her head, as if more for security than ornament. Brown was also the prevailing tint of her eyebrows, thickly-set eyelashes, and eyes, and was even suggested in the slight sallowness of her complexion. But her lips were well-cut and fresh-colored and her hands and feet small and finely formed. She would have passed for a pretty girl, had she not suggested something more.

She sat down, and began to examine a pile of papers before her with that concentration and attention to detail which was characteristic of her eyes, pausing at times with prettily knit brows, and her penholder between her lips, in the semblance of a pout that was pleasant enough to see. Suddenly the rattle of hoofs and wheels struck her with the sense of something forgotten, and she put down her work quickly and stood up listening. The sound of rough voices and her father's querulous accents was broken upon by a cultivated and more familiar utterance: "All right; I'll speak to her at once. Wait there," and the door opened to the well-known physician of Burnt Ridge, Dr. Duchesne.

" Look here," he said, with an abruptness that was only saved from being brusque by a softer intonation and a reassuring smile, " I met Miguel helping an accident into your buggy. Your orders, eh ? "

" Oh, yes, " said Josephine, quietly. " A man I saw on the road."

" Well, it 's a bad case, and wants prompt attention. And as your house is the nearest I came with him here."

" Certainly," she said gravely. " Take him to the second room beyond — Steve's room — it 's ready," she explained to two dusky shadows in the hall behind the doctor.

" And look here," said the doctor, partly closing the door behind him and regarding her with critical eyes, " you always said you 'd like to see some of my queer cases. Well, this is one — a serious one, too ; in fact, it 's just touch and go with him. There 's a piece of the bone pressing on the brain no bigger than that, but as much as if all Burnt Ridge was atop of him ! I 'm going to lift it. I want somebody here to stand by, some one who can lend a hand with a sponge, eh ? — some one who is n't going to faint or scream, or even shake a hair's-breadth. eh ? "

The color rose quickly to the girl's cheek, and her eyes kindled. " I 'll come," she said thoughtfully. " Who is he ?"

The doctor stared slightly at the unessential query. " Don't know, — one of the river miners, I reckon. It's an urgent case. I 'll go and get everything ready. You 'd better," he added, with an ominous glance at her gray frock, " put something over your dress." The suggestion made her grave, but did not alter her color.

A moment later she entered the room. It was the one that had always been set apart for her brother: the very bed on which the unconscious man lay had been arranged that morning with her own hands. Something of this passed through her mind as she saw that the doctor had wheeled it beneath the strong light in the centre of the room, stripped its outer coverings with professional thoughtfulness, and rearranged the mattresses. But it did not seem like the same room. There was a pungent odor in the air from some freshly-opened phial; an almost feminine neatness and luxury in an open morocco case like a jewel box on the table, shining with spotless steel. At the head of the bed one of her own servants, the powerful mill foreman, was assisting with the mingled curiosity and *blasé* experience of one accustomed to smashed and lacerated digits. At first she did not look at the central unconscious figure on the bed, whose sufferings seemed to her to have been vicariously transferred to the concerned, eager, and drawn faces that looked down upon its immunity. Then she femininely recoiled before the bared white neck and shoulders displayed above the quilt, until, forcing herself to look upon the face half-concealed by bandages and the head from which the dark tangles of hair had been ruthlessly sheared, she began to share the doctor's unconcern in his personality. What mattered who or what *he* was? It was — a case!

The operation began. With the same earnest intelligence that she had previously shown, she quickly and noiselessly obeyed the doctor's whispered orders, and even half anticipated them. She was conscious of a singular curiosity that, far from being mean or ignoble, seemed to lift her not only above the ordinary weaknesses of her own sex, but made her superior to the men around her. Almost before she knew it, the operation

was over, and she regarded with equal curiosity the ostentatious solicitude with which
the doctor seemed to be wiping his fateful
instrument that bore an odd resemblance to
a silver-handled centre-bit. The stertorous
breathing below the bandages had given way
to a fainter but more natural respiration.
There was a moment of suspense. The doctor's hand left the pulse and lifted the closed
eyelid of the sufferer. A slight movement
passed over the figure. The sluggish face
had cleared ; life seemed to struggle back
into it before even the dull eyes participated
in the glow. Dr. Duchesne with a sudden
gesture waved aside his companions, but not
before Josephine had bent her head eagerly
forward.

" He is coming to," she said.

At the sound of that deep clear voice —
the first to break the hush of the room —
the dull eyes leaped up, and the head turned
in its direction. The lips moved and uttered
a single rapid sentence. The girl recoiled.

" You 're all right now," said the doctor,
cheerfully, intent only upon the form before
him.

The lips moved again, but this time feebly
and vacantly ; the eyes were staring vaguely
around.

" What's matter ? What's all about ? "
said the man, thickly.

" You 've had a fall. Think a moment.
Where do you live ? "

Again the lips moved, but this time only
to emit a confused, incoherent murmur. Dr.
Duchesne looked grave, but recovered himself quickly.

" That will do. Leave him alone now,"
he said brusquely to the others.

But Josephine lingered.

" He spoke well enough just now," she
said eagerly. " Did you hear what he
said ? "

" Not exactly," said the doctor, abstractedly, gazing at the man.

" He said : ' You 'll have to kill me
first,' " said Josephine, slowly.

" Humph ; " said the doctor, passing his
hand backwards and forwards before the
man's eyes to note any change in the staring
pupils.

" Yes," continued Josephine, gravely. " I
suppose," she added, cautiously, "he was
thinking of the operation — of what you
had just done to him ? "

" What *I* had done to him ? Oh, yes ! "

CHAPTER II.

BEFORE noon the next day it was known throughout Burnt Ridge Valley that Dr. Duchesne had performed a difficult operation upon an unknown man, who had been picked up unconscious from a fall, and carried to Burnt Ridge Ranch. But although the unfortunate man's life was saved by the operation, he had only momentarily recovered consciousness — relapsing into a semi-idiotic state, which effectively stopped the discovery of any clue to his friends or his identity. As it was evidently an *accident*, which, in that rude community — and even in some more civilized ones — conveyed a vague impression of some contributary incapacity on the part of the victim, or some Providential interference of a retributive character, Burnt Ridge gave itself little trouble about it. It is unnecessary to say that Mr. and Mrs. Forsyth gave themselves and Josephine much more. They had a theory and a grievance. Satisfied from the first that the alleged victim was a drunken tramp, who submitted to have a hole bored in his head in order to foist himself upon the ranch, they were loud in their protests, even hinting at a conspiracy between Josephine and the stranger to supplant her brother in the property, as he had already in the spare bedroom. " Did n't all that yer happen *the very night* she pretended to go for Stephen — eh?" said Mrs. Forsyth. " Tell me that! And did n't she have it all arranged with the buggy to bring him here, as that sneaking doctor let out — eh? Looks mighty curious, don't it?" she muttered darkly to the old man. But although that gentleman, even from his own selfish view, would scarcely have submitted to a surgical operation and later idiocy as the price of insuring comfortable dependency, he had no doubt others were base enough to do it; and lent a willing ear to his wife's suspicions.

Josephine's personal knowledge of the stranger went little further. Doctor Duchesne had confessed to her his professional disappointment at the incomplete results of the operation. He had saved the man's life, but as yet not his reason. There was still hope, however, for the diagnosis revealed nothing that might prejudice a favorable progress. It was a most interesting case. He would watch it carefully, and as soon as the patient could be removed would take him to the county hospital, where, under his own eyes, the poor fellow would have the benefit of the latest science and the highest specialists. Physically, he was doing remarkably well; indeed, he must have been a fine young chap, free from blood taint or vicious complication, whose flesh had healed like an infant's. It should be recorded that it was at this juncture that Mrs. Forsyth first learnt that a *silver plate* let into the artful stranger's skull was an adjunct of the healing process! Convinced that this infamous extravagance was part and parcel of the conspiracy, and was only the beginning of other assimilations of the Forsyths' metallic substance; that the plate was probably polished and burnished with a fulsome inscription to the doctor's skill, and would pass into the possession and adornment of a perfect stranger, her rage knew no bounds. He or his friends ought to be made to pay for it or work it out! In vain it was declared that a few dollars were all that was found in the man's pocket, and that no memoranda gave any indication of his name, friends, or history beyond the suggestion that he came from a distance. This was clearly a part of the conspiracy! Even Josephine's practical good sense was obliged to take note of this singular absence of all record regarding him, and the apparent obliteration of everything that might be responsible for his ultimate fate.

Homeless, friendless, helpless, and even nameless, the unfortunate man of twenty-five was thus left to the tender mercies of the mistress of Burnt Ridge Ranch, as if he had been a new-born foundling laid at her door. But this mere claim of weakness was not all ; it was supplemented by a singular personal appeal to Josephine's nature. From the time that he turned his head towards her voice on that fateful night, his eyes had always followed her around the room with a wondering, yearning, canine half-intelligence. Without being able to convince herself that he understood her better than his regular attendant furnished by the doctor, she could not fail to see that he obeyed her implicitly, and that whenever any difficulty arose between him and his nurse she was always appealed to. Her pride in this proof

of her practical sovereignty was flattered;
and when Doctor Duchesne finally admitted
that although the patient was now physically
able to be removed to the hospital, yet he
would lose in the change that very strong
factor which Josephine had become in his
mental recovery, the young girl as frankly
suggested that he should stay as long as there
was any hope of restoring his reason. Doctor Duchesne was delighted. With all his
enthusiasm for science, he had a professional
distrust of some of its disciples, and perhaps
was not sorry to keep this most interesting
case in his own hands. To him her suggestion was only a womanly kindness, tempered
with womanly curiosity. But the astonishment and stupefaction of her parents at this
evident corroboration of suspicions they had
as yet only half believed was tinged with
superstitious dread. Had she fallen in love
with this helpless stranger? or, more awful
to contemplate, was he really no stranger,
but a surreptitious lover thus strategically
brought under her roof? For once they refrained from open criticism. The very mag-
nitude of their suspicions left them dumb.

It was thus that the virgin Chatelaine of
Burnt Ridge Ranch was left to gaze un-

trammeled upon her pale and handsome
guest, whose silken, bearded lips and sad,
childlike eyes might have suggested a more
Exalted Sufferer in their absence of any
suggestion of a grosser material manhood.
But even this imaginative appeal did not
enter into her feelings. She felt for her
good-looking, helpless patient a profound
and honest pity. I do not know whether
she had ever heard that "pity was akin to
love." She would probably have resented
that utterly untenable and atrocious common-
place. There was no suggestion, real or illu-
sive, of any previous masterful quality in the
man which might have made his present de-
pendent condition picturesque by contrast.
He had come to her handicapped by an
unromantic accident and a practical want of
energy and intellect. He would have to
touch her interest anew if, indeed, he would
ever succeed in dispelling the old impression.
His beauty, in a community of picturesquely
handsome men, had little weight with her,
except to accent the contrast with their fuller
manhood.

Her life had given her no illusions in regard to the other sex. She had found them,
however, more congenial and safer compan-

ions than women, and more accessible to her
own sense of justice and honor. In return,
they had respected and admired rather than
loved her, in spite of her womanly graces.
If she had at times contemplated eventual
marriage, it was only as a possible practical
partnership in her business; but as she lived
in a country where men thought it dishonor-
able and a proof of incompetency to rise by
their wives' superior fortune, she had been
free from that kind of mercenary persecu-
tion, even from men who might have wor-
shiped her in hopeless and silent honor.

For this reason, there was nothing in the
situation that suggested a single compromising speculation in the minds of the neighbors, or disturbed her own tranquillity.
There seemed to be nothing in the future
except a possible relief to her curiosity.
Some day the unfortunate man's reason
would be restored, and he would tell his
simple history. Perhaps he might explain
what was in his mind when he turned to her
the first evening with that singular sentence
which had often recurred strangely to her,
she knew not why. It did not strike her
until later that it was because it had been
the solitary indication of an energy and

capacity that seemed unlike him. Nevertheless, after that explanation, she would have been quite willing to have shaken hands with him and parted.

And yet — for there was an unexpressed remainder in her thought — she was never entirely free or uninfluenced in his presence. The flickering vacancy of his sad eyes sometimes became fixed with a resolute immobility under the gentle questioning with which she had sought to draw out his faculties, that both piqued and exasperated her. He could say " Yes " and " No," as she thought, intelligently, but he could not utter a coherent sentence nor write a word, except like a child in imitation of his copy. She taught him to repeat after her the names of the inanimate objects in the room, then the names of the doctor, his attendant, the servant, and, finally, her own under her Christian prenomen, with frontier familiarity; but when she pointed to himself he waited for *her* to name him! In vain she tried him with all the masculine names she knew; his was not one of them, or he would not or could not speak it. For at times she rejected the professional dictum of the doctor that the faculty of memory was wholly paralyzed or held in abeyance, even to the half-automatic recollection of his letters, yet she inconsistently began to teach him the alphabet with the same method, and — in her sublime unconsciousness of his manhood — with the same discipline as if he were a very child. When he had recovered sufficiently to leave his room, she would lead him to the porch before her window, and make him contented and happy by allowing him to watch her at work at her desk, occasionally answering his wondering eyes with a word, or stirring his faculties with a question. I grieve to say that her parents had taken advantage of this publicity and his supposed helpless condition to show their disgust of his assumption, to the extreme of making faces at him — an act which he resented with such a furious glare that they retreated hurriedly to their own veranda. A fresh though somewhat inconsistent grievance was added to their previous indictment of him : " If we ain't found dead in our bed with our throats cut by that woman's crazy husband " (they had settled by this time that there had been a clandestine marriage), " we'll be lucky," groaned Mrs. Forsyth.

Meantime, the mountain summer waxed

to its fullness of fire and fruition. There
were days when the crowded forest seemed
choked and impeded with its own foliage,
and pungent and stifling with its own rank
maturity; when the long hillside ranks of
wild oats, thickset and impassable, filled the
air with the heated dust of germination. In
this quickening irritation of life it would be
strange if the unfortunate man's torpid intellect was not helped in its awakening, and
he was allowed to ramble at will over the
ranch; but with the instinct of a domestic
animal he always returned to the house, and
sat in the porch, where Josephine usually
found him awaiting her when she herself returned from a visit to the mill. Coming
thence one day she espied him on the mountain-side leaning against a projecting ledge
in an attitude so rapt and immovable that
she felt compelled to approach him. He
appeared to be dumbly absorbed in the
prospect, which might have intoxicated a
saner mind.

Half veiled by the heat that rose quiver-
ingly from the fiery cañon below, the domain
of Burnt Ridge stretched away before him,
until, lifted in successive terraces hearsed
and plumed with pines, it was at last lost in

the ghostly snow-peaks. But the practical
Josephine seized the opportunity to try once
more to awaken the slumbering memory of
her pupil. Following his gaze with signs
and questions, she sought to draw from him
some indication of familiar recollection of
certain points of the map thus unrolled behind him. But in vain. She even pointed
out the fateful shadow of the overhanging
ledge on the road where she had picked him
up — there was no response in his abstracted
eyes. She bit her lips; she was becoming
irritated again. Then it occurred to her
that, instead of appealing to his hopeless
memory, she had better trust to some unre-
flective automatic instinct independent of it,
and she put the question a little forward:
" When you leave us, where will you go from
here?" He stirred slightly, and turned towards her. She repeated her query slowly
and patiently, with signs and gestures recognized between them. A faint glow of intelligence struggled into his eyes; he lifted
his arm slowly, and pointed.

" Ah! those white peaks — the Sierras?"
she asked, eagerly. No reply. " Beyond
them?"

" Yes."

"The States?" No reply. "Further still?"

He remained so patiently quiet and still pointing that she leaned forward, and, following with her eyes the direction of his hand, saw that he was pointing to the sky!

Then a great quiet fell upon them. The whole mountain-side seemed to her to be hushed, as if to allow her to grasp and realize for the first time the pathos of the ruined life at her side, which *it* had known so long, but which she had never felt till now. The tears came to her eyes; in her swift revulsion of feeling she caught the thin uplifted hand between her own. It seemed to her that he was about to raise them to his lips, but she withdrew them hastily, and moved away. She had a strange fear that if he had kissed them, it might seem as if some dumb animal had touched them — or — *it might not.* The next day she felt a consciousness of this in his presence, and a wish that he was well-cured and away. She determined to consult Dr. Duchesne on the subject when he next called.

But the doctor, secure in the welfare of his patient, had not visited him lately, and she found herself presently absorbed in the business of the ranch, which at this season was particularly trying. There had also been a quarrel between Dick Shipley, her mill foreman, and Miguel, her ablest and most trusted vaquero, and in her strict sense of impartial justice she was obliged to side on the merits of the case with Shipley against her oldest retainer. This troubled her, as she knew that with the Mexican nature, fidelity and loyalty were not unmixed with quick and unreasoning jealousy. For this reason she was somewhat watchful of the two men when work was over, and there was a chance of their being thrown together. Once or twice she had remained up late to meet Miguel returning from the posada at San Ramon, filled with *aguardiente* and a recollection of his wrongs, and to see him safely bestowed before she herself retired. It was on one of those occasions, however, that she learned that Dick Shipley, hearing that Miguel had disparaged him freely at the posada, had broken the discipline of the ranch, and absented himself the same night that Miguel "had leave," with a view of facing his antagonist on his own ground. To prevent this, the fearless girl at once secretly set out alone to overtake and bring back the delinquent.

For two or three hours the house was thus left to the sole occupancy of Mr. and Mrs. Forsyth and the invalid — a fact only dimly suspected by the latter, who had become vaguely conscious of Josephine's anxiety, and had noticed the absence of light and movement in her room. For this reason, therefore, having risen again and mechanically taken his seat in the porch to await her return, he was startled by hearing *her* voice in the shadow of the lower porch, accompanied by a hurried tapping against the door of the old couple. The half-reasoning man arose, and would have moved towards it, but suddenly he stopped rigidly, with white and parted lips and vacantly distended eyeballs.

Meantime the voice and muffled tapping had brought the tremulous fingers of old Forsyth to the door-latch. He opened the door partly; a slight figure that had been lurking in the shadow of the porch pushed rapidly through the opening. There was a faint outcry quickly hushed, and the door closed again. The rays of a single candle showed the two old people hysterically clasping in their arms the figure that had entered — a slight but vicious-looking young fellow of five-and-twenty.

" There, d—n it ! " he said impatiently, in a voice whose rich depth was like Josephine's, but whose querulous action was that of the two. old people before him, " let me go, and quit that. I did n't come here to be strangled ! I want some money — money, you hear ! Devilish quick, too, for I 've got to be off again before daylight. So look sharp, will you ? "

" But, Stevy dear, when you did n't come that time three months ago, but wrote from Los Angeles, you said you 'd made a strike at last, and " —

" What are you talking about ? " he interrupted violently. " That was just my lyin' to keep you from worryin' me. Three months ago — three months ago ! Why, you must have been crazy to have swallowed it; I had n't a cent."

" Nor have we," said the old woman, shrilly. " That hellish sister of yours still keeps us like beggars. Our only hope was you, our own boy. And now you only come to — to go again."

" But *she* has money; *she's* doing well, and *she* shall give it to me," he went on, angrily. " She can't bully me with her business airs and morality. Who else has

got a right to share, if it is not her own
brother ? "

Alas for the fatuousness of human malev-
olence ! Had the unhappy couple related
only the simple facts they knew about the
new guest of Burnt Ridge Ranch, and the
manner of his introduction, they might have
spared what followed.

But the old woman broke into a vindictive cry: " Who else, Steve — who else ?
Why, the slut has brought a *man* here —
a sneaking, deceitful, underhanded, crazy
lover ! "

" Oh, has she ? " said the young man,
fiercely, yet secretly pleased at this promising evidence of his sister's human weakness.
" Where is she ? I 'll go to her. She 's in
her room, I suppose," and before they could
restrain him, he had thrown off their im-
peding embraces and darted across the
hall.

The two old people stared doubtfully at
each other. For even this powerful ally,
whose strength, however, they were by no
means sure of, might succumb before the
determined Josephine ! Prudence demanded
a middle course. " Ain't they brother and
sister ? " said the old man, with an air

of virtuous toleration. "Let 'em fight it out."

The young man impatiently entered the room he remembered to have been his sister's. By the light of the moon that streamed upon the window he could see she was not there. He passed hurriedly to the door of her bedroom; it was open; the room was empty, the bed unturned. She was not in the house — she had gone to the mill. Ah! What was that they had said? An infamous thought passed through the scoundrel's mind. Then, in what he half believed was an access of virtuous fury, he began by the dim light to rummage in the drawers of the desk for such loose coin or valuables as, in the perfect security of the ranch, were often left unguarded. Suddenly he heard a heavy footstep on the threshold, and turned.

An awful vision — a recollection, so unexpected, so ghostlike in that weird light that he thought he was losing his senses — stood before him. It moved forwards with staring eyeballs and white and open lips from which a horrible inarticulate sound issued that was the speech of no living man! With a single desperate, almost superhuman effort Stephen

Forsyth bounded aside, leaped from the window, and ran like a madman from the house. Then the apparition trembled, collapsed, and sank in an undistinguishable heap to the ground.

When Josephine Forsyth returned an hour later with her mill foreman, she was startled to find her helpless patient in a fit on the floor of her room. With the assistance of her now converted and penitent employee, she had the unfortunate man conveyed to his room — but not until she had thoughtfully rearranged the disorder of her desk and closed the open drawers without attracting Dick Shipley's attention. In the morning, hearing that the patient was still in the semi-conscious exhaustion of his late attack, but without seeing him, she sent for Dr. Duchesne. The doctor arrived while she was absent at the mill, where, after a careful examination of his patient, he sought her with some little excitement.

" Well ? " she said, with eager gravity.

" Well, it looks as if your wish would be gratified. Your friend has had an epileptic fit, but the physical shock has started his mental machinery again. He has recovered his faculties; his memory is returning: he thinks and speaks coherently ; he is as sane as you and I."

" And " — said Josephine, questioning the doctor's knitted eyebrows.

" I am not yet sure whether it was the result of some shock he does n't remember ; or an irritation of the brain, which would indicate that the operation had not been successful and that there was still some physical pressure or obstruction there — in which case he would be subject to these attacks all his life."

" Do you think his reason came before the fit or after ? " asked the girl, anxiously.

" I could n't say. Had anything happened ? "

" I was away, and found him on the floor on my return," she answered, half uneasily. After a pause she said, " Then he has told you his name and all about himself ? "

" Yes, it 's nothing at all ! He was a stranger just arrived from the States, going to the mines — the old story ; had no near relations, of course ; was n't missed or asked after ; remembers walking along the ridge and falling over ; name, John Baxter, of Maine." He paused, and relaxing into a slight smile, added, " I have n't spoiled your romance, have I ? "

" No," she said, with an answering smile. Then as the doctor walked briskly away she slightly knitted her pretty brows, hung her head, patted the ground with her little foot beyond the hem of her gown, and said to herself, " The man was lying to him."

CHAPTER III.

On her return to the house, Josephine apparently contented herself with receiving the bulletin of the stranger's condition from the servant, for she did not enter his room. She had obtained no theory of last night's incident from her parents, who, beyond a querulous agitation that was quickened by the news of his return to reason, refrained from even that insidious comment which she half feared would follow. When another day passed without her seeing him, she nevertheless was conscious of a little embarrassment when his attendant brought her the request that she would give him a moment's speech in the porch, whither he had been removed.

She found him physically weaker; indeed, so much so that she was fain, even in her embarrassment, to assist him back to the bench from which he had ceremoniously risen. But she was so struck with the change in his face and manner, a change so virile and masterful, in spite of its gentle

sadness of manner, that she recoiled with a
slight timidity as if he had been a stranger,
although she was also conscious that he
seemed to be more at his ease than she
was. He began in a low exhausted voice,
but before he had finished his first sentence, she felt herself in the presence of a
superior.

"My thanks come very late, Miss Forsyth," he said, with a faint smile, "but no
one knows better than yourself the reason
why, or can better understand that they
mean that the burden you have so generously taken on yourself is about to be lifted.
I know all, Miss Forsyth. Since yesterday
I have learned how much I owe you, even
my life I believe, though I am afraid I must
tell you in the same breath that *that* is of
little worth to any one. You have kindly
helped and interested yourself in a poor
stranger who turns out to be a nobody, without friends, without romance, and without
even mystery. You found me lying in the
road down yonder, after a stupid accident
that might have happened to any other careless tramp, and which scarcely gave me a
claim to a bed in the county hospital, much
less under this kindly roof. It was not my

fault, as you know, that all this did not come out sooner; but while it does n't lessen your generosity, it does n't lessen my debt, and although I cannot hope to ever repay you, I can at least keep the score from running on. Pardon my speaking so bluntly, but my excuse for speaking at all was to say 'Good-by' and 'God bless you.' Dr. Duchesne has promised to give me a lift on my way in his buggy when he goes."

There was a slight touch of consciousness in his voice in spite of its sadness, which struck the young girl as a weak and even ungentlemanly note in his otherwise self-abnegating and undemonstrative attitude. If he was a common tramp, he would n't talk in that way, and if he was n't, why did he lie? Her practical good sense here asserted itself.

"But you are far from strong yet; in fact, the doctor says you might have a relapse at any moment, and you have — that is, you *seem* to have no money," she said gravely.

"That 's true," he said, quickly. "I remember I was quite played out when I entered the settlement, and I think I had parted from even some little trifles I carried with me. I am afraid I was a poor find to those who picked me up, and you ought to have taken warning. But the doctor has offered to lend me enough to take me to San Francisco, if only to give a fair trial to the machine he has set once more a-going."

"Then you have friends in San Francisco?" said the young girl quickly. "Those who know you? Why not write to them first, and tell them you are here?"

"I don't think your postmaster here would be preoccupied with letters for John Baxter, if I did," he said, quietly. "But here is the doctor waiting. Good-by."

He stood looking at her in a peculiar, yet half-resigned way, and held out his hand. For a moment she hesitated. Had he been less independent and strong, she would have refused to let him go — have offered him some slight employment at the ranch; for oddly enough, in spite of the suspicion that he was concealing something, she felt that she would have trusted him, and he would have been a help to her. But he was not only determined, but *she* was all the time conscious that he was a totally different man from the one she had taken care of, and merely ordinary prudence demanded that she

should know something more of him first.
She gave him her hand constrainedly; he
pressed it warmly.

Dr. Duchesne drove up, helped him into
the buggy, smiled a good-natured but half-
perfunctory assurance that he would look
after " her patient," and drove away.

The whole thing was over, but so unexpectedly, so suddenly, so unromantically, so
unsatisfactorily, that, although her common
sense told her that it was perfectly natural,
proper, business-like, and reasonable, and,
above all, final and complete, she did not
know whether to laugh or be angry. Yet
this was her parting from the man who had
but a few days ago moved her to tears with
a single hopeless gesture. Well, this would
teach her what to expect. Well, what had
she expected? Nothing!

Yet for the rest of the day she was un-
reasonably irritable, and, if the conjointure
be not paradoxical, severely practical, and
inhumanly just. Falling foul of some pre-
sumption of Miguel's, based upon his pre-
scriptive rights through long service on the
estate, with the recollection of her severity
towards his antagonist in her mind, she rated
that trusted retainer with such pitiless equity

and unfeminine logic that his hot Latin blood chilled in his veins, and he stood livid on the road. Then, informing Dick Shipley with equally relentless calm that she might feel it necessary to change *all* her foremen unless they could agree in harmony, she sought the dignified seclusion of her castle. But her respected parents, whose triumphant relief at the stranger's departure had emboldened them to await her return in their porch with bended bows of invective and lifted javelins of aggression, recoiled before the resistless helm of this cold-browed Minerva, who galloped contemptuously past them.

Nevertheless, she sat late that night at her desk. The cold moon looked down upon her window, and lit up the empty porch where her silent guest had mutely watched her. For a moment she regretted that he had recovered his reason, excusing herself on the practical ground that he would never have known his dependence, and he would have been better cared for by her. She felt restless and uneasy. This slight divergence from the practical groove in which her life had been set had disturbed her in many other things, and given her the first views of the narrowness of it.

Suddenly she heard a step in the porch.
The lateness of the hour, perhaps some other
reason, seemed to startle her, and she half
rose. The next moment the figure of Miguel
appeared at the doorway, and with a quick,
hurried look around him, and at the open
window, he approached her. He was evidently under great excitement, his hollow
shaven cheek looked like a waxen effigy in
the mission church; his yellow, tobacco-
stained eye glittered like phosphorescent
amber, his lank gray hair was damp and
perspiring; but more striking than this was
the evident restraint he had put upon himself, pressing his broad-brimmed sombrero
with both of his trembling yellow hands
against his breast. The young girl cast a
hurried glance at the open window and at
the gun which stood in the corner, and then
confronted him with clear and steady eyes,
but a paler cheek.

Ah, he began in Spanish, which he himself
had taught her as a child, it was a strange
thing, his coming there to-night; but, then,
mother of God! it was a strange, a terrible
thing that she had done to him — old Miguel,
her uncle's servant: he that had known her
as a *muchacha;* he that had lived all his

life at the ranch — ay, and whose fathers before him had lived there all *their* lives and driven the cattle over the very spot where she now stood, before the thieving Americans came here! But he would be calm; yes, the señora should find him calm, even as she was when she told him to go. He would not speak. No, he — Miguel — would contain himself; yes, he *had* mastered himself, but could he restrain others? Ah, yes, *others* — that was it. Could he keep Manuel and Pepe and Dominguez from talking to the milkman — that leaking sieve, that gabbling brute of a Shipley, for whose sake she had cast off her old servant that very day?

She looked at him with cold astonishment, but without fear. Was he drunk with *aguardiente*, or had his jealousy turned his brain? He continued gasping, but still pressing his hat against his breast.

Ah, he saw it all! Yes, it was to-day, the day he left. Yes, she had thought it safe to cast Miguel off now — now that *he* was gone!

Without in the least understanding him, the color had leaped to her cheek, and the consciousness of it made her furious.

" How dare you ? " she said, passionately. " What has that stranger to do with my affairs or your insolence ? "

He stopped and gazed at her with a certain admiring loyalty. " Ah ! so," he said, with a deep breath, " the señora is the niece of her uncle. She does well not to fear *him* — a dog," — with a slight shrug, — " who is more than repaid by the señora's condescension. *He* dare not speak ! "

" Who dare not speak ? Are you mad ? " She stopped with a sudden terrible instinct of apprehension. " Miguel," she said in her deepest voice, " answer me, I command you ! Do you know anything of this man ? "

It was Miguel's turn to recoil from his mistress. " Ah, my God ! is it possible the señora has not suspect ? "

" Suspect ! " said Josephine, haughtily, albeit her proud heart was beating quickly. " I *suspect* nothing. I command you to tell me what you *know*."

Miguel turned with a rapid gesture and closed the door. Then, drawing her away from the window, he said in a hurried whisper, —

" I know that that man has not the name of Baxter ! I know that he has the name of

Randolph, a young gambler, who have won a large sum at Sacramento, and, fearing to be robbed by those he won of, have walk to himself through the road in disguise of a miner. I know that your brother Esteban have decoyed him here, and have fallen on him."

"Stop!" said the young girl, her eyes, which had been fixed with the agony of conviction, suddenly flashing with the energy of despair. "And you call yourself the servant of my uncle, and dare say this of his nephew?"

"Yes, señora," broke out the old man, passionately. "It is because I am the servant of your uncle that I, and I *alone*, dare say it to you! It is because I perjured my soul, and have perjured my soul to deny it elsewhere, that I now dare to say it! It is because I, your servant, knew it from one of my countrymen, who was of the gang, — because I, Miguel, knew that your brother was not far away that night, and because I, whom you would dismiss, have picked up this pocket-book of Randolph's and your brother's ring which he have dropped, and I have found beneath the body of the man you sent me to fetch."

He drew a packet from his bosom, and tossed it on the desk before her.

" And why have you not told me this before? " said Josephine, passionately.

Miguel shrugged his shoulders.

" What good? Possibly this dog Randolph would die. Possibly he would live — as a lunatic. Possibly would happen what has happened! The señora is beautiful. The American has eyes. If the Doña Josephine's beauty shall finish what the silly Don Esteban's arm have begun — what matter? "

" Stop! " cried Josephine, pressing her hands across her shuddering eyes. Then, uncovering her white and set face, she said rapidly, " Saddle my horse and your own at once. Then take your choice! Come with me and repeat all that you have said in the presence of that man, or leave this ranch forever. For if I live I shall go to him tonight, and tell the whole story."

The old man cast a single glance at his mistress, shrugged his shoulders, and, without a word, left the room. But in ten minutes they were on their way to the county town.

Day was breaking over the distant Burnt Ridge — a faint, ghostly level, like a funeral pall, in the dim horizon — as they drew up before the gaunt, white-painted pile of the hospital building. Josephine uttered a cry. Dr. Duchesne's buggy was before the door. On its very threshold they met the doctor, dark and irritated. " Then you heard the news? " he said, quickly.

Josephine turned her white face to the doctor's. " What news? " she asked, in a voice that seemed strangely deep and resonant.

" The poor fellow had another attack last night, and died of exhaustion about an hour ago. I was too late to save him."

" Did he say anything? Was he conscious? " asked the girl, hoarsely.

" No; incoherent! Now I think of it, he harped on the same string as he did the night of the operation. What was it he said? you remember."

" ' You 'll have to kill me first,' " repeated Josephine, in a choking voice.

" Yes; something about his dying before he 'd tell. Well, he came back to it before he went off — they often do. You seem a little hoarse with your morning ride. You should take care of that voice of yours. By the way, it's a good deal like your brother's."

. . . .

The Chatelaine of Burnt Ridge never married.

THROUGH THE SANTA CLARA WHEAT.

CHAPTER I.

It was an enormous wheat-field in the Santa Clara valley, stretching to the horizon line unbroken. The meridian sun shone upon it without glint or shadow; but at times, when a stronger gust of the trade winds passed over it, there was a quick slanting impression of the whole surface that was, however, as unlike a billow as itself was unlike a sea. Even when a lighter zephyr played down its long level, the agitation was superficial, and seemed only to momentarily lift a veil of greenish mist that hung above its immovable depths. Occasional puffs of dust alternately rose and fell along an imaginary line across the field, as if a current of air were passing through it, but were otherwise inexplicable.

Suddenly a faint shout, apparently somewhere in the vicinity of the line, brought out a perfectly clear response, followed by the audible murmur of voices, which it was impossible to localize. Yet the whole field was so devoid of any suggestion of human life or motion that it seemed rather as if the vast expanse itself had become suddenly articulate and intelligible.

" Wot say ? "

" Wheel off."

" Whare ? "

" In the road."

One of the voices here indicated itself in the direction of the line of dust, and said, " Comin'," and a man stepped out from the wheat into a broad and dusty avenue.

With his presence three things became apparent.

First, that the puffs of dust indicated the existence of the invisible avenue through the unlimited and unfenced field of grain; secondly, that the stalks of wheat on either side of it were so tall as to actually hide a passing vehicle ; and thirdly, that a vehicle had just passed, had lost a wheel, and been dragged partly into the grain by its frightened horse, which a dusty man was trying to restrain and pacify.

The horse, given up to equine hysterics, and evidently convinced that the ordinary buggy behind him had been changed into some dangerous and appalling creation, still plunged and kicked violently to rid himself of it. The man who had stepped out of the depths of the wheat quickly crossed the road, unhitched the traces, drew back the vehicle, and, glancing at the traveler's dusty and disordered clothes, said, with curt sympathy : —

" Spilt, too ; but not hurt, eh ? "

" No, neither of us.   I went over with the buggy when the wheel cramped, but *she* jumped clear."

He made a gesture indicating the presence of another. The man turned quickly. There was a second figure, a young girl standing beside the grain from which he had emerged, embracing a few stalks of wheat with one arm and a hand in which she still held her parasol, while she grasped her gathered skirts with the other, and trying to find a secure foothold for her two neat narrow slippers on a crumbling cake of adobe above the fathomless dust of the roadway. Her face, although annoyed and discontented, was pretty, and her light dress and slim figure were suggestive of a certain superior condition.

The man's manner at once softened with Western courtesy. He swung his broad-brimmed hat from his head, and bent his body with the ceremoniousness of the country ball-room. "I reckon the lady had better come up to the shanty out o' the dust and sun till we kin help you get these things fixed," he said to the driver. "I'll send round by the road for your hoss, and have one of mine fetch up your wagon."

"Is it far?" asked the girl, slightly acknowledging his salutation, without waiting for her companion to reply.

"Only a step this way," he answered, motioning to the field of wheat beside her.

"What! In *there?* I never could go in there," she said, decidedly.

"It's a heap shorter than by the road, and not so dusty. I'll go with you, and pilot you."

The young girl cast a vexed look at her companion as the probable cause of all this trouble, and shook her head. But at the same moment one little foot slipped from the adobe into the dust again. She instantly clambered back with a little feminine shriek,

and ejaculated: " Well, of all things! " and
then, fixing her blue annoyed eyes on the
stranger, asked impatiently, " Why could n't
I go there by the road 'n the wagon? I
could manage to hold on and keep in."

" Because I reckon you 'd find it too
pow'ful hot waitin' here till we got round
to ye."

There was no doubt it was very hot; the
radiation from the baking roadway beating
up under her parasol, and pricking her
cheekbones and eyeballs like needles. She
gave a fastidious little shudder, furled her
parasol, gathered her skirts still tighter,
faced about, and said, " Go on, then." The
man slipped backwards into the ranks of
stalks, parting them with one hand, and
holding out the other as if to lead her. But
she evaded the invitation by holding her
tightly-drawn skirt with both hands, and
bending her head forward as if she had not
noticed it. The next moment the road, and
even the whole outer world, disappeared behind them, and they seemed floating in a
choking green translucent mist.

But the effect was only momentary; a
few steps further she found that she could
walk with little difficulty between the ranks

of stalks, which were regularly spaced, and
the resemblance now changed to that of a
long pillared conservatory of greenish glass,
that touched all objects with its pervading
hue. She also found that the close air above
her head was continually freshened by the
interchange of currents of lower temperature from below, — as if the whole vast field
had a circulation of its own, — and that the
adobe beneath her feet was gratefully cool
to her tread. There was no dust, as he had
said ; what had at first half suffocated her
seemed to be some stimulating aroma of
creation that filled the narrow green aisles,
and now imparted a strange vigor and excitement to her as she walked along. Meantime her guide was not conversationally idle.
Now, no doubt, she had never seen anything
like this before ? It was ordinary wheat,
only it was grown on adobe soil — the rich-
est in the valley. These stalks, she could
see herself, were ten and twelve feet high.
That was the trouble, they all ran too much
to stalk, though the grain yield was " suthen'
pow'ful." She could tell that to her friends,
for he reckoned she was the only young lady
that had ever walked under such a growth.
Perhaps she was new to Californy ? He

thought so from the start. Well, this was
Californy, and this was not the least of the
ways it could "lay over" every other country on God's yearth. Many folks thought
it was the gold and the climate, but she could
see for herself what it could do with wheat.
He wondered if her brother had ever told
her of it? No, the stranger was n't her
brother. Nor cousin, nor company? No;
only the hired driver from a San José hotel,
who was takin' her over to Major Randolph's. Yes, he knew the old major; the
ranch was a pretty place, nigh unto three
miles further on. Now that he knew the
driver was no relation of hers he did n't
mind telling her that the buggy was a
"rather old consarn," and the driver did n't
know his business. Yes, it might be fixed
up so as to take her over to the major's;
there was one of their own men — a young
fellow — who could do anything that *could*
be done with wood and iron, — a reg'lar
genius! — and *he 'd* tackle it. It might take
an hour, but she 'd find it quite cool waiting
in the shanty. It was a rough place, for
they only camped out there during the season to look after the crop, and lived at their
own homes the rest of the time. Was she

going to stay long at the major's? He noticed she had not brought her trunk with
her. Had she known the major's wife long?
Perhaps she thought of settling in the neigh-
borhood?

All this naïve, good-humored questioning
— so often cruelly misunderstood as mere
vulgar curiosity, but as often the courteous
instinct of simple unaffected people to enter-
tain the stranger by inviting him to talk
of what concerns himself rather than their
own selves — was nevertheless, I fear, met
only by monosyllables from the young lady
or an impatient question in return. She
scarcely raised her eyes to the broad jean-
shirted back that preceded her through the
grain until the man abruptly ceased talking,
and his manner, without losing its half-pater-
nal courtesy, became graver. She was beginning to be conscious of her incivility, and
was trying to think of something to say,
when he exclaimed with a slight air of relief,
"Here we are!" and the shanty suddenly
appeared before them.

It certainly was very rough — a mere shell
of unpainted boards that scarcely rose above
the level of the surrounding grain, and a few
yards distant was invisible. Its slightly slop-

ing roof, already warped and shrunken into long fissures that permitted glimpses of the steel-blue sky above, was evidently intended only as a shelter from the cloudless sun in those two months of rainless days and dewless nights when it was inhabited. Through the open doors and windows she could see a row of "bunks," or rude sleeping berths against the walls, furnished with coarse mattresses and blankets. As the young girl halted, the man with an instinct of delicacy hurried forward, entered the shanty, and dragging a rude bench to the doorway, placed it so that she could sit beneath the shade of the roof, yet with her back to these domestic revelations. Two or three men, who had been apparently lounging there, rose quietly, and unobtrusively withdrew. Her guide brought her a tin cup of deliciously cool water, exchanged a few hurried words with his companions, and then disappeared with them, leaving her alone.

Her first sense of relief from their company was, I fear, stronger than any other feeling. After a hurried glance around the deserted apartment, she arose, shook out her dress and mantle, and then going into the darkest corner supported herself with one hand against the wall while with the other she drew off, one by one, her slippers from her slim, striped-stockinged feet, shook and blew out the dust that had penetrated within, and put them on again. Then, perceiving a triangular fragment of looking-glass nailed against the wall, she settled the strings of her bonnet by the aid of its reflection, patted the fringe of brown hair on her forehead with her separated five fingers as if playing an imaginary tune on her brow, and came back with maidenly abstraction to the doorway.

Everything was quiet, and her seclusion seemed unbroken. A smile played for an instant in the soft shadows of her eyes and mouth as she recalled the abrupt withdrawal of the men. Then her mouth straightened and her brows slightly bent. It was certainly very unmannerly in them to go off in that way. "Good heavens! could n't they have stayed around without talking? Surely it did n't require four men to go and bring up that wagon!" She picked up her parasol from the bench with an impatient little jerk. Then she held out her ungloved hand into the hot sunshine beyond the door with the gesture she would have used had it been raining, and withdrew it as quickly — her hand quite scorched in the burning rays. Nevertheless, after another impatient pause she desperately put up her parasol and stepped from the shanty.

Presently she was conscious of a faint sound of hammering not far away. Perhaps there was another shed, but hidden, like everything else, in this monotonous, ridiculous grain. Some stalks, however, were trodden down and broken around the shanty; she could move more easily and see where she was going. To her delight, a few steps further brought her into a current of the trade-wind and a cooler atmosphere. And a short distance beyond them, certainly, was the shed from which the hammering proceeded. She approached it boldly.

It was simply a roof upheld by rude uprights and crossbeams, and open to the breeze that swept through it. At one end was a small blacksmith's forge, some machinery, and what appeared to be part of a small steam-engine. Midway of the shed was a closet or cupboard fastened with a large padlock. Occupying its whole length on the other side was a work-bench, and at the further end stood the workman she had heard.

He was apparently only a year or two older than herself, and clad in blue jean overalls, blackened and smeared with oil and coal-dust. Even his youthful face, which he turned towards her, had a black smudge running across it and almost obliterating a small auburn moustache. The look of surprise that he gave her, however, quickly passed; he remained patiently and in a half-preoccupied way, holding his hammer in his hand, as she advanced. This was evidently the young fellow who could "do anything that could be done with wood and iron."

She was very sorry to disturb him, but could he tell her how long it would be before the wagon could be brought up and mended? He could not say that until he himself saw what was to be done; if it was only a matter of the wheel he could fix it up in a few moments; if, as he had been told, it was a case of twisted or bent axle, it would take longer, but it would be here very soon. Ah, then, would he let her wait here, as she was very anxious to know at once, and it was much cooler than in the shed? Certainly; he would go over and bring her a bench. But here she begged he would n't trouble himself, she could sit anywhere comfortably.

The lower end of the work-bench was covered with clean and odorous shavings; she lightly brushed them aside and, with a youthful movement, swung herself to a seat upon it, supporting herself on one hand as she leaned towards him. She could thus see that his eyes were of a light-yellowish brown, like clarified honey, with a singular look of clear concentration in them, which, however, was the same whether turned upon his work, the surrounding grain, or upon her. This, and his sublime unconsciousness of the smudge across his face and his blackened hands, made her wonder if the man who could do everything with wood and iron was above doing anything with water. She had half a mind to tell him of it, particularly as she noticed also that his throat below the line of sunburn disclosed by his open collar was quite white, and his grimy hands well made. She was wondering whether he would be affronted if she said in her politest way, " I beg your pardon, but do you know you have quite accidentally got something on your face," and offer her handkerchief, which, of course, he would decline, when her eye fell on the steam-engine.

" How odd ! Do you use that on the farm ? "

" No," — he smiled here, the smudge ac-
centing it and setting off his white teeth in
a Christy Minstrel fashion that exasperated
her — no, although it *could* be used, and had
been.   But it was his first effort, made two
years ago, when he was younger and more
inexperienced.   It was a rather rough thing,
she could see — but he had to make it at
odd times with what iron he could pick up
or pay for, and at different forges where he
worked.

She begged his pardon — where —

Where he worked.

Ah, then he was the machinist or engineer here ?

No, he worked here just like the others,
only he was allowed to put up a forge while
the grain was green, and have his bench in
consideration of the odd jobs he could do in
the way of mending tools, etc.   There was a
heap of mending and welding to do — she
had no idea how quickly agricultural ma-
chines got out of order!   He had done much
of his work on the steam-engine on moonlit
nights.   Yes; she had no idea how perfectly
clear and light it was here in the valley on
such nights ; although of course the shadows
were very dark, and when he dropped a

screw or a nut it was difficult to find. He had worked there because it saved time and because it did n't cost anything, and he had nobody to look on or interfere with him. No, it was not lonely; the coyotes and wild cats sometimes came very near, but were always more surprised and frightened than he was; and once a horseman who had strayed off the distant road yonder mistook him for an animal and shot at him twice.

He told all this with such freedom from embarrassment and with such apparent unconsciousness of the blue eyes that were following him, and the light, graceful figure, — which was so near his own that in some of his gestures his grimy hands almost touched its delicate garments, — that, accustomed as she was to a certain masculine aberration in her presence, she was greatly amused by his naïve acceptance of her as an equal. Suddenly, looking frankly in her face, he said:

"I 'll show you a secret, if you care to see it."

Nothing would please her more.

He glanced hurriedly around, took a key from his pocket, and unlocked the padlock that secured the closet she had noticed. Then, reaching within, with infinite care he brought out a small mechanical model.

"There's an invention of my own. A reaper and thresher combined. I'm going to have it patented and have a big one made from this model. This will work, as you see."

He then explained to her with great precision how as it moved over the field the double operation was performed by the same motive power. That it would be a saving of a certain amount of labor and time which she could not remember. She did not understand a word of his explanations; she saw only a clean and pretty but complicated toy that under the manipulation of his grimy fingers rattled a number of frail-like staves and worked a number of wheels and drums, yet there was no indication of her ignorance in her sparkling eyes and smiling, breathless attitude. Perhaps she was interested in his own absorption; the revelation of his preoccupation with this model struck her as if he had made her a confidante of some boyish passion for one of her own sex, and she regarded him with the same sympathizing superiority.

"You will make a fortune out of it," she said pleasantly.

Well, he might make enough to be able

to go on with some other inventions he had
in his mind. They cost money and time, no
matter how careful one was.

This was another interesting revelation to
the young girl. He not only did not seem
to care for the profit his devotion brought
him, but even his one beloved ideal might
be displaced by another. So like a man,
after all!

Her reflections were broken upon by the
sound of voices. The young man carefully
replaced the model in its closet with a parting glance as if he was closing a shrine, and
said, "There comes the wagon." The young
girl turned to face the men who were dragging it from the road, with the half-compla-
cent air of having been victorious over their
late rude abandonment, but they did not
seem to notice it or to be surprised at her
companion, who quickly stepped forward and
examined the broken vehicle with workman-
like deliberation.

"I hope you will be able to do something
with it," she said sweetly, appealing directly
to him. "I should thank you *so much.*"

He did not reply. Presently he looked
up to the man who had brought her to the
shanty, and said, "The axle's strained, but

it 's safe for five or six miles more of this
road. I 'll put the wheel on easily." He
paused, and without glancing at her, continued, " You might send her on by the cart."

" Pray don't trouble yourselves," interrupted the young girl, with a pink uprising
in her cheeks ; " I shall be quite satisfied
with the buggy as it stands." Send her on
in the cart, indeed! Really, they were a
rude set — *all* of them."

Without taking the slightest notice of her
remark, the man replied gravely to the young
mechanic, " Yes, but we 'll be wanting the
cart before it can get back from taking
her."

" Her " again. " I assure you the buggy
will serve perfectly well — if this — gentleman — will only be kind enough to put on
the wheel again," she returned hotly.

The young mechanic at once set to work.
The young girl walked apart silently until the
wheel was restored to its axle. But to her
surprise a different horse was led forward to
be harnessed.

" We thought your horse was n't safe in
case of another accident," said the first man,
with the same smileless consideration. " This
one would n't cut up if he was harnessed to

an earthquake or a worse driver than you 've got."

It occurred to her instantly that the more obvious remedy of sending another driver had been already discussed and rejected by them. Yet, when her own driver appeared a moment afterwards, she ascended to her seat with some dignity and a slight increase of color.

" I am very much obliged to you all," she said, without glancing at the young inventor.

" Don't mention it, miss."

" Good afternoon."

" Good afternoon." They all took off their hats with the same formal gravity as the horse moved forward, but turned back to their work again before she was out of the field.

CHAPTER II.

THE ranch of Major Randolph lay on a rich *falda* of the Coast Range, and over-looked the great wheat plains that the young girl had just left. The house of wood and adobe, buried to its first story in rose-trees and passion vines, was large and commodi-ous. Yet it contained only the major, his wife, her son and daughter, and the few oc-casional visitors from San Francisco whom he entertained, and she tolerated.

For the major's household was not entirely harmonious. While a young infantry sub-altern at a Gulf station, he had been at-tracted by the piquant foreign accent and dramatic gestures of a French Creole widow, and — believing them, in the first flush of his youthful passion more than an offset to the encumbrance of her two children who, with the memory of various marital infideli-ties were all her late husband had left her — had proposed, been accepted, and promptly married to her. Before he obtained his captaincy, she had partly lost her accent, and those dramatic gestures, which had accented the passion of their brief courtship, began to intensify domestic altercation and the bursts of idle jealousy to which she was subject. Whether she was revenging herself on her second husband for the faults of her first is not known, but it was certain that she brought an unhallowed knowledge of the weaknesses, cheap cynicism, and vanity of a foreign predecessor, to sit in judgment upon the simple-minded and chivalrous American soldier who had succeeded him, and who was, in fact, the most loyal of husbands. The natural result of her skepticism was an espionage and criticism of the wives of the major's brother officers that compelled a frequent change of quarters. When to this was finally added a racial divergence and antipathy, the public disparagement of the customs and education of her female colleagues, and the sudden insistence of a foreign and French dominance in her household beyond any ordinary Creole justification, Randolph, presumably to avoid later international complications, resigned while he was as yet a major. Luckily his latest banishment to an extreme Western outpost had placed him in California during the flood of a speculation epoch. He purchased a valuable Spanish grant to three leagues of land for little over a three months' pay. Following that yearning which compels retired ship-captains and rovers of all degrees to buy a farm in their old days, the major, professionally and socially inured to border strife, sought surcease and Arcadian repose in ranching.

It was here that Mrs. Randolph, late relict of the late Scipion L'Hommadieu, devoted herself to bringing up her children after the extremest of French methods, and in resurrecting a "*de*" from her own family to give a distinct and aristocratic character to their name. The "*de Fontanges l'Hommadieu*" were, however, only known to their neighbors, after the Western fashion, by their stepfather's name, — when they were known at all — which was seldom. For the boy was unpleasantly conceited as a precocious worldling, and the girl as unpleasantly complacent in her *rôle* of *ingénue*. The household was completely dominated by Mrs. Randolph. A punctilious Catholic, she attended all the functions of the adjacent mission, and the shadow of a black *soutane* at twilight gliding through the wild oat-fields behind the ranch had often been mistaken for a coyote. The peace-loving major did not object to a piety which, while it left his own conscience free, imparted a respectable religious air to his household, and kept him from the equally distasteful approaches of the Puritanism of his neighbors, and was blissfully unconscious that he was strengthening the antagonistic foreign element in his family with an alien church.

Meantime, as the repaired buggy was slowly making its way towards his house, Major Randolph entered his wife's boudoir with a letter which the San Francisco post had just brought him. A look of embarrassment on his good-humored face strengthened the hard lines of hers; she felt some momentary weakness of her natural enemy, and prepared to give battle.

"I'm afraid here's something of a muddle, Josephine," he began with a deprecating smile. "Mallory, who was coming down here with his daughter, you know"—

"This is the first intimation *I* have had that anything has been settled upon," interrupted the lady, with appalling deliberation.

"However, my dear, you know I told you

last week that he thought of bringing her here while he went South on business. You know, being a widower, he has no one to leave her with."

"And I suppose it is the American fashion to intrust one's daughters to any old boon companions?"

"Mallory is an old friend," interrupted the major, impatiently. "He knows I'm married, and although he has never seen *you*, he is quite willing to leave his daughter here."

"Thank you!"

"Come, you know what I mean. The man naturally believes that my wife will be a proper chaperone for his daughter. But that is not the present question. He intended to call here; I expected to take you over to San José to see her and all that, you know; but the fact of it is — that is — it seems from this letter that — he's been called away sooner than he expected, and that — well — hang it! the girl is actually on her way here now."

"Alone?"

"I suppose so. You know one thinks nothing of that here."

"Or any other propriety, for that matter."

"For heaven's sake, Josephine, don't be ridiculous! Of course it's stupid her coming in this way, and Mallory ought to have brought her — but she's coming, and we must receive her. By Jove! Here she is now!" he added, starting up after a hurried glance through the window. "But what kind of a d—d turn-out is that, anyhow?"

It certainly was an odd-looking conveyance that had entered the gates, and was now slowly coming up the drive towards the house. A large draught horse harnessed to a dust-covered buggy, whose strained fore-axle, bent by the last mile of heavy road, had slanted the tops of the fore-wheels towards each other at an alarming angle. The light, graceful dress and elegant parasol of the young girl, who occupied half of its single seat, looked ludicrously pronounced by the side of the slouching figure and grimy duster of the driver, who occupied the other half.

Mrs. Randolph gave a gritty laugh. "I thought you said she was alone. Is that an escort she has picked up, American fashion, on the road?"

"That's her hired driver, no doubt. Hang it! she can't drive here by herself," retorted the major, impatiently, hurrying to the door and down the staircase. But he was instantly followed by his wife. She had no idea of permitting a possible understanding to be exchanged in their first greeting. The late M. l'Hommadieu had been able to impart a whole plan of intrigue in a single word and glance.

Happily, Rose Mallory, already in the hall, in a few words detailed the accident that had befallen her, to the honest sympathy of the major and the coldly-polite concern of Mrs. Randolph, who, in deliberately chosen sentences, managed to convey to the young girl the conviction that accidents of any kind to young ladies were to be regarded as only a shade removed from indiscretions. Rose was impressed, and even flattered, by the fastidiousness of this foreign-appearing woman, and after the fashion of youthful natures, accorded to her the respect due to recognized authority. When to this authority, which was evident, she added a depreciation of the major, I fear that some common instinct of feminine tyranny responded in Rose's breast, and that on the very threshold of the honest soldier's home she tacitly agreed with the wife to look down upon him. Mrs.

Randolph departed to inform her son and daughter of their guest's arrival. As a matter of fact, however, they had already observed her approach to the house through the slits of their drawn window-blinds, and those even narrower prejudices and limited comprehensions which their education had fostered. The girl, Adele, had only grasped the fact that Rose had come to their house in fine clothes, alone with a man, in a broken-down vehicle, and was moved to easy mirth and righteous wonder. The young man, Emile, had agreed with her, with the mental reservation that the guest was pretty, and must eventually fall in love with him. They both, however, welcomed her with a trained politeness and a superficial attention that, while the indifference of her own country-men in the wheat-field was still fresh in her recollection, struck her with grateful contrast; the major's quiet and unobtrusive kindliness naturally made less impression, or was accepted as a matter of course.

"Well," said the major, cheerfully but tentatively, to his wife when they were alone again, "she seems a nice girl, after all; and a good deal of pluck and character, by Jove! to push on in that broken buggy rather than linger or come in a farm cart, eh?"

"She was alone in that wheat-field," said Mrs. Randolph, with grim deliberation, "for half an hour; she confesses it herself — *talking with a young man!*"

"Yes, but the others had gone for the buggy. And, in the name of Heaven, what would you have her do — hide herself in the grain?" said the major, desperately. "Besides," he added, with a recklessness he afterwards regretted, "that mechanical chap they've got there is really intelligent and worth talking to."

"I have no doubt *she* thought so," said Mrs. Randolph, with a mirthless smile. "In fact, I have observed that the American freedom generally means doing what you *want* to do. Indeed, I wonder she did n't bring him with her! Only I beg, major, that you will not again, in the presence of my daughter, — and I may even say, of my son, — talk lightly of the solitary meetings of young ladies with mechanics, even though their faces were smutty, and their clothes covered with oil."

The major here muttered something about there being less danger in a young lady listening to the intelligence of a coarsely-dressed laborer than to the compliments of

a rose-scented fop, but Mrs. Randolph walked
out of the room before he finished the evident platitude.

That night Rose Mallory retired to her
room in a state of self-satisfaction that she
even felt was to a certain extent a virtue.
She was delighted with her reception and
with her hostess and family. It was strange
her father had not spoken more of *Mrs.*
Randolph, who was clearly the superior of
his old friend. What fine manners they all
had, so different from other people she had
known! There was quite an Old World civilization about them; really, it was like going
abroad! She would make the most of her
opportunity and profit by her visit. She
would begin by improving her French; they
spoke it perfectly, and with such a pure accent. She would correct certain errors she
was conscious of in her own manners, and
copy Mrs. Randolph as much as possible.
Certainly, there was a great deal to be said
of Mrs. Randolph's way of looking at things.
Now she thought of it calmly, there *was* too
much informality and freedom in American
ways! There was not enough respect due
to position and circumstances. Take those
men in the wheat-field, for example. Yet

here she found it difficult to formulate an indictment against them for " freedom." She would like to go there some day with the Randolphs and let them see what company manners were ! She was thoroughly convinced now that her father had done wrong in sending her alone ; it certainly was most disrespectful to them and careless of him (she had quite forgotten that she had herself proposed to her father to go alone rather than wait at the hotel), and she must have looked very ridiculous in her fine clothes and the broken-down buggy. When her trunk came by express to-morrow she would look out something more sober. She must remember that she was in a Catholic and religious household now. Ah, yes ! how very fine it was to see that priest at dinner in his *soutane*, sitting down like one of the family, and making them all seem like a picture of some historical and aristocratic romance ! And then they were actually " *de Fontanges l'Hommadieu.*" How different he was from that shabby Methodist minister who used to come to see her father in a black cravat with a hideous bow ! Really there was something to say for a religion that contained so much picturesque refinement ; and for her part —

but that will do. I beg to say that I am not writing of any particular snob or feminine monstrosity, but of a very charming creature, who was quite able to say her prayers afterwards like a good girl, and lay her pretty cheek upon her pillow without a blush.

She opened her window and looked out. The moon, a great silver dome, was uplifting itself from a bluish-gray level, which she knew was the distant plain of wheat. Somewhere in its midst appeared a dull star, at times brightening as if blown upon or drawn upwards in a comet-like trail. By some odd instinct she felt that it was the solitary forge of the young inventor, and pictured him standing before it with his abstracted hazel eyes and a face more begrimed in the moonlight than ever. When *did* he wash himself? Perhaps not until Sunday. How lonely it must be out there! She slightly shivered and turned from the window. As she did so, it seemed to her that something knocked against her door from without. Opening it quickly, she was almost certain that the sound of a rustling skirt retreated along the passage. It was very late; perhaps she had disturbed the house by shut-

ting her window. No doubt it was the motherly interest of Mrs. Randolph that impelled her to come softly and look after her ;
and for once her simple surmises were correct. For not only the inspecting eyes of
her hostess, but the amatory glances of the
youthful Emile, had been fastened upon her
window until the light disappeared, and even
the Holy Mission Church of San José had
assured itself of the dear child's safety with
a large and supple ear at her keyhole.

The next morning Major Randolph took
her with Adele in a light cariole over the
ranch. Although his domain was nearly as
large as the adjoining wheat plain, it was
not, like that, monopolized by one enormous
characteristic yield, but embraced a more
diversified product. There were acres and
acres of potatoes in rows of endless and
varying succession ; there were miles of wild
oats and barley, which overtopped them as
they drove in narrow lanes of dry and dusty
monotony ; there were orchards of pears,
apricots, peaches, and nectarines, and vineyards of grapes, so comparatively dwarfed
in height that they scarcely reached to the
level of their eyes, yet laden and breaking
beneath the weight of their ludicrously dis-

proportionate fruit. What seemed to be a vast green plateau covered with tiny patches, that headed the northern edge of the prospect, was an enormous bed of strawberry plants. But everywhere, crossing the track, bounding the fields, orchards, and vineyards, intersecting the paths of the whole domain, were narrow irrigating ducts and channels of running water.

"Those," said the major, poetically, "are the veins and arteries of the ranch. Come with me now, and I 'll show you its pulsating heart." Descending from the wagon into pedestrian prose again, he led Rose a hundred yards further to a shed that covered a wonderful artesian well. In the centre of a basin a column of water rose regularly with the even flow and volume of a brook. "It is one of the largest in the State," said the major, "and is the life of all that grows here during six months of the year."

Pleased as the young girl was with those evidences of the prosperity and position of her host, she was struck, however, with the fact that the farm-laborers, wine-growers, nurserymen, and all field hands scattered on the vast estate were apparently of the same independent, unpastoral, and unprofessional character as the men of the wheat-field. There were no cottages or farm buildings that she could see, nor any apparent connection between the household and the estate; far from suggesting tenantry or retainers, the men who were working in the fields glanced at them as they passed with the indifference of strangers, or replied to the major's greetings or questionings with perfect equality of manner, or even business-like reserve and caution. Her host explained that the ranch was worked by a company "on shares;" that those laborers were, in fact, the bulk of the company; and that he, the major, only furnished the land, the seed, and the implements. "That man who was driving the long roller, and with whom you were indignant because he would n't get out of our way, is the president of the company."

"That need n't make him so uncivil," said Rose, poutingly, "for if it comes to that you 're the *landlord*," she added triumphantly.

"No," said the major, good-humoredly. "I am simply the man driving the lighter and more easily-managed team for pleasure, and he 's the man driving the heavier and more difficult machine for work. It's for me to get out of his way; and looked at in the light of my being *the landlord* it is still worse, for as we're working 'on shares' I'm interrupting *his* work, and reducing *his* profits merely because I choose to sacrifice my own."

I need not say that those atrociously leveling sentiments were received by the young ladies with that feminine scorn which is only qualified by misconception. Rose, who, under the influence of her hostess, had a vague impression that they sounded something like the French Revolution, and that Adele must feel like the Princess Elizabeth, rushed to her relief like a good girl. " But, major, now, *you're* a gentleman, and if *you* had been driving that roller, you know you would have turned out for us."

" I don't know about that," said the major, mischievously; " but if I had, I should have known that the other fellow who accepted it wasn't a gentleman."

But Rose, having sufficiently shown her partisanship in the discussion, after the feminine fashion, did not care particularly for the logical result. After a moment's silence she resumed: " And the wheat ranch below — is that carried on in the same way?"

"Yes. But their landlord is a bank, who advances not only the land, but the money to work it, and does n't ride around in a buggy with a couple of charmingly distracting young ladies."

"And do they all share alike?" continued Rose, ignoring the pleasantry, "big and little — that young inventor with the rest?"

She stopped. She felt the *ingénue's* usually complacent eyes suddenly fixed upon her with an unhallowed precocity, and as quickly withdrawn. Without knowing why, she felt embarrassed, and changed the subject.

The next day they drove to the Convent of Santa Clara and the Mission College of San José. Their welcome at both places seemed to Rose to be a mingling of caste greeting and spiritual zeal, and the austere seclusion and reserve of those cloisters repeated that suggestion of an Old World civilization that had already fascinated the young Western girl. They made other excursions in the vicinity, but did not extend it to a visit to their few neighbors. With their reserved and exclusive ideas this fact did not strike Rose as peculiar, but on a later shopping expedition to the town of San José, a certain reticence and aggressive sensitiveness on the part of the shopkeepers and tradespeople towards the Randolphs produced an unpleasant impression on her mind. She could not help noticing, too, that after the first stare of astonishment which greeted her appearance with her hostess, she herself was included in the antagonism. With her youthful prepossession for her friends, this distinction she regarded as flattering and aristocratic, and I fear she accented it still more by discussing with Mrs. Randolph the merits of the shopkeepers' wares in school-girl French before them. She was unfortunate enough, however, to do this in the shop of a polyglot German.

"Oxcoos me, mees," he said gravely, — "but dot lady speeks Engeleesh so goot mit yoursclluf, and ven you dells to her dot silk is hallf gotton in English, she onderstand you mooch better, and it don't make nodings to me." The laugh which would have followed from her own countrywomen did not, however, break upon the trained faces of the "*de Fontanges l'Hommadieus*," yet while Rose would have joined in it, albeit a little ruefully, she felt for the first time mortified at their civil insincerity.

At the end of two weeks, Major Randolph received a letter from Mr. Mallory. When he had read it, he turned to his wife: " He thanks you," he said, " for your kindness to his daughter, and explains that his sudden departure was owing to the necessity of his taking advantage of a great opportunity for speculation that had offered." As Mrs. Randolph turned away with a slight shrug of the shoulders, the major continued: " But you have n't heard all! That opportunity was the securing of a half interest in a Cinnabar lode in Sonora, which has already gone up a hundred thousand dollars in his hands! By Jove! a man can afford to drop a little social ceremony on those terms — eh, Josephine?" he concluded with a triumphant chuckle.

" He 's as likely to lose his hundred thousand to-morrow, while his manners will remain," said Mrs. Randolph. " I 've no faith in these sudden California fortunes! "

" You 're wrong as regards Mallory, for he 's as careful as he is lucky. He don't throw money away for appearance sake, or he 'd have a rich home for that daughter. He could afford it."

Mrs. Randolph was silent. " She is his

only daughter, I believe," she continued presently.

"Yes — he has no other kith or kin," returned the major.

"She seems to be very much impressed by Emile," said Mrs. Randolph.

Major Randolph faced his wife quickly.

"In the name of all that's ridiculous, my dear, you are not already thinking of" — he gasped.

"I should be very loth to give *my* sanction to anything of the kind, knowing the difference of her birth, education, and religion, — although the latter I believe she would readily change," said Mrs. Randolph, severely. "But when you speak of *my* already thinking of 'such things,' do you suppose that your friend, Mr. Mallory, did n't consider all that when he sent that girl here?"

"Never," said the major, vehemently, "and if it entered his head now, by Jove, he'd take her away to-morrow — always supposing I did n't anticipate him by sending her off myself."

Mrs. Randolph uttered her mirthless laugh. "And you suppose the girl would go? Really, major, you don't seem to understand this boasted liberty of your own countrywoman. What does she care for her father's control? Why, she 'd make him do just what *she* wanted. But," she added with an expression of dignity, "perhaps we had better not discuss this until we know something of Emile's feelings in the matter. That is the only question that concerns us." With this she swept out of the room, leaving the major at first speechless with honest indignation, and then after the fashion of all guileless natures, a little uneasy and suspicious of his own guilelessness. For a day or two after, he found himself, not without a sensation of meanness, watching Rose when in Emile's presence, but he could distinguish nothing more than the frank satisfaction she showed equally to the others. Yet he found himself regretting even that, so subtle was the contagion of his wife's suspicions.

CHAPTER III.

IT had been a warm morning; an unusual mist, which the sun had not dissipated, had crept on from the great grain-fields beyond, and hung around the house charged with a dry, dusty closeness that seemed to be quite independent of the sun's rays, and more like a heated exhalation or emanation of the soil itself. In its acrid irritation Rose thought she could detect the breath of the wheat as on the day she had plunged into its pale, green shadows. By the afternoon this mist had disappeared, apparently in the same mysterious manner, but not scattered by the usual trade-wind, which — another unusual circumstance — that day was not forthcoming. There was a breathlessness in the air like the hush of listening expectancy, which filled the young girl with a vague restlessness, and seemed to even affect a scattered company of crows in the field beyond the house, which rose suddenly with startled but aimless wings, and then dropped vacantly among the grain again.

Major Randolph was inspecting a distant part of the ranch, Mrs. Randolph was presumably engaged in her boudoir, and Rose was sitting between Adele and Emile before the piano in the drawing-room, listlessly turning over the leaves of some music. There had been an odd mingling of eagerness and abstraction in the usual attentions of the young man that morning, and a certain nervous affectation in his manner of twisting the ends of a small black moustache, which resembled his mother's eyebrows, that had affected Rose with a half-amused, half-uneasy consciousness, but which she had, however, referred to the restlessness produced by the weather. It occurred to her also that the vacuously amiable Adele had once or twice regarded her with the same precocious, child-like curiosity and infantine cunning she had once before exhibited. All this did not, however, abate her admiration for both — perhaps particularly for this picturesquely gentlemanly young fellow, with his gentle audacities of compliment, his caressing attentions, and his unfailing and equal address. And when, discovering that she had mislaid her fan for the fifth time that morning, he started up with equal and undiminished fire to go again and fetch it, the look of grateful pleasure and pleading perplexity in her pretty eyes might have turned a less conceited brain than his.

" But you don't know where it is ! "

" I shall find it by instinct."

" You are spoiling me — you two." The parenthesis was a hesitating addition, but she continued, with fresh sincerity, " I shall be quite helpless when I leave here — if I am ever able to go by myself."

" Don't ever go, then."

" But just now I want my fan ; it is so close everywhere to-day."

" I fly, mademoiselle."

He started to the door.

She called after him : —

" Let me help your instinct, then ; I had it last in the major's study."

" That was where I was going."

He disappeared. Rose got up and moved uneasily towards the window. " How queer and quiet it looks outside. It 's really too bad that he should be sent after that fan again. He 'll never find it." She resumed her place at the piano, Adele following her with round, expectant eyes. After a pause she started up again. " I 'll go and fetch it myself," she said, with a half-embarrassed laugh, and ran to the door.

Scarcely understanding her own nervousness, but finding relief in rapid movement, Rose flew lightly up the staircase. The major's study, where she had been writing letters, during his absence, that morning, was at the further end of a long passage, and near her own bedroom, the door of which, as she passed, she noticed, half-abstractedly, was open, but she continued on and hurriedly entered the study. At the same moment Emile, with a smile on his face, turned towards her with the fan in his hand.

"Oh, you've found it," she said, with nervous eagerness. " I was so afraid you'd have all your trouble for nothing."

She extended her hand, with a half-breathless smile, for the fan, but he caught her outstretched little palm in his own, and held it.

"Ah! but you are not going to leave us, are you?"

In a flash of consciousness she understood him, and, as it seemed to her, her own nervousness, and all, and everything. And with it came a swift appreciation of all it meant to her and her future. To be always with him and like him, a part of this refined and restful seclusion — akin to all that had so attracted her in this house ; not to be obliged to educate herself up to it, but to be in it on equal terms at once; to know that it was no wild, foolish youthful fancy, but a wise, thoughtful, and prudent resolve, that her father would understand and her friends respect: these were the thoughts that crowded quickly upon her, more like an explanation of her feelings than a revelation, in the brief second that he held her hand. It was not, perhaps, love as she had dreamed it, and even *believed* it, before. She was not ashamed or embarrassed ; she even felt, with a slight pride, that she was not blushing. She raised her eyes frankly. What she *would* have said she did not know, for the door, which he had closed behind her, began to shake violently.

It was not the fear of some angry intrusion or interference surely that made him drop her hand instantly. It was not — her second thought — the idea that some one had fallen in a fit against it that blanched his face with abject and unreasoning terror! It must have been something else that caused him to utter an inarticulate cry and dash out of the room and down the stairs like a madman! What had happened?

In her own self-possession she knew that all this was passing rapidly, that it was not the door now that was still shaking, for it had swung almost shut again — but it was the windows, the book-shelves, the floor beneath her feet, that were all shaking. She heard a hurried scrambling, the trampling of feet below, and the quick rustling of a skirt in the passage, as if some one had precipitately fled from her room. Yet no one had called to her — even *he* had said nothing. Whatever had happened they clearly had not cared for her to know.

The jarring and rattling ceased as suddenly, but the house seemed silent and empty. She moved to the door, which had now swung open a few inches, but to her astonishment it was fixed in that position, and she could not pass. As yet she had been free from any personal fear, and even now it was with a half smile at her imprisonment in the major's study, that she rang the bell and turned to the window. A man, whom she recognized as one of the ranch laborers, was standing a hundred feet away in the garden, looking curiously at the house. He saw her face as she tried to raise the sash, uttered an exclamation, and ran forward. But before she could understand what he said, the sash began to rattle in her hand, the jarring recommenced, the floor shook beneath her feet, a hideous sound of grinding seemed to come from the walls, a thin seam of dust-like smoke broke from the ceiling, and with the noise of falling plaster a dozen books followed each other from the shelves, in what in the frantic hurry of that moment seemed a grimly deliberate succession; a picture hanging against the wall, to her dazed wonder, swung forward, and appeared to stand at right angles from it; she felt herself reeling against the furniture; a deadly nausea overtook her; as she glanced despairingly towards the window, the outlying fields beyond the garden seemed to be undulating like a sea. For the first time she raised her voice, not in fear, but in a pathetic little cry of apology for her awkwardness in tumbling about and not being able to grapple this new experience, and then she found herself near the door, which had once more swung free. She grasped it eagerly, and darted out of the study into the deserted passage. Here some instinct made her follow the line of the wall, rather than the shaking balusters of the corridor and staircase, but before she reached the bottom she heard a shout, and the farm laborer she had seen coming towards her seized her by the arm, dragged her to the open doorway of the drawing-room, and halted beneath its arch in the wall. Another thrill, but lighter than before, passed through the building, then all was still again.

" It 's over ; I reckon that 's all just now," said the man, coolly. " It 's quite safe to cut and run for the garden now, through this window." He half led, half lifted her through the French window to the veranda and the ground, and locking her arm in his, ran quickly forward a hundred feet from the house, stopping at last beneath a large post oak where there was a rustic seat into which she sank. " You 're safe now, I reckon," he said grimly.

She looked towards the house ; the sun was shining brightly ; a cool breeze seemed to have sprung up as they ran. She could see a quantity of rubbish lying on the roof from which a dozen yards of zinc gutter were perilously hanging ; the broken shafts of the further cluster of chimneys, a pile of bricks scattered upon the ground and among the battered down beams of the end of the veranda — but that was all. She lifted her now whitened face to the man, and with the apologetic smile still lingering on her lips, asked : —

" What does it all mean ? What has happened ? "

The man stared at her. " D' ye mean to say ye don't know ? "

" How could I ? They must have all left the house as soon as it began. I was talking to — to M. l'Hommadieu, and he suddenly left."

The man brought his face angrily down within an inch of her own. " D' ye mean to say that them d—d French half-breeds stampeded and left yer there alone ? "

She was still too much stupefied by the reaction to fully comprehend his meaning, and repeated feebly with her smile still faintly lingering : " But you don't tell me *what* it was ? "

" An earthquake," said the man, roughly, " and if it had lasted ten seconds longer it would have shook the whole shanty down and left you under it. Yer kin tell *that* to them, if they don't know it, but from the way they made tracks to the fields, I reckon they did. They 're coming now."

Without another word he turned away half surlily, half defiantly, passing scarce fifty yards away Mrs. Randolph and her daughter, who were hastening towards their guest.

" Oh, here you are! " said Mrs. Randolph, with the nearest approach to effusion that Rose had yet seen in her manner. " We were wondering where you had run to, and were getting quite concerned. Emile was looking for you everywhere."

The recollection of his blank and abject face, his vague outcry and blind fright, came back to Rose with a shock that sent a flash of sympathetic shame to her face. The ingenious Adele noticed it, and dutifully pinched her mother's arm.

" Emile ? " echoed Rose faintly — " looking for *me?* "

Mother and daughter exchanged glances.

" Yes," said Mrs. Randolph, cheerfully, " he says he started to run with you, but you got ahead and slipped out of the garden door — or something of the kind," she added, with the air of making light of Rose's girlish fears. "You know one scarcely knows what one does at such times, and it must have been frightfully strange to *you* — and he's been quite distracted, lest you should have wandered away. Adele, run and tell him Miss Mallory has been here under the oak all the time."

Rose started — and then fell hopelessly back in her seat. Perhaps it *was* true! Perhaps he had not rushed off with that awful face and without a word. Perhaps she herself had been half-frightened out of her reason. In the simple, weak kindness of her nature it seemed less dreadful to believe that the fault was partly her own.

"And you went back into the house to look for us when all was over," said Mrs. Randolph, fixing her black, beady, magnetic eyes on Rose, "and that stupid yokel Zake brought you out again. He need n't have clutched your arm so closely, my dear, — I must speak to the major about his excessive familiarity — but I suppose I shall be told that that is American freedom. I call it 'a liberty.'"

It struck Rose that she had not even thanked the man — in the same flash that she remembered something dreadful that he had said. She covered her face with her hands and tried to recall herself.

Mrs. Randolph gently tapped her shoulder with a mixture of maternal philosophy and discipline, and continued: "Of course, it's an upset — and you're confused still. That's nothing. They say, dear, it's perfectly well known that no two people's recollections of these things ever are the same. It's really ridiculous the contradictory stories one hears. Isn't it, Emile?"

Rose felt that the young man had joined them and was looking at her. In the fear that she should still see some trace of the startled, selfish animal in his face, she did not dare to raise her eyes to his, but looked at his mother. Mrs. Randolph was standing then, collected but impatient.

"It's all over now," said Emile, in his usual voice, "and except the chimneys and some fallen plaster there's really no damage done. But I'm afraid they have caught it pretty badly at the mission, and at San Francisco in those tall, flashy, rattle-trap buildings they're putting up. I've just sent off one of the men for news."

Her father was in San Francisco by that time; and she had never thought of *him!*

In her quick remorse she now forgot all else and rose to her feet.

"I must telegraph to my father at once," she said hurriedly ; "he is there."

"You had better wait until the messenger returns and hear his news," said Emile. "If the shock was only a slight one in San Francisco, your father might not understand you, and would be alarmed."

She could see his face now — there was no record of the past expression upon it, but he was watching her eagerly. Mrs. Randolph and Adele had moved away to speak to the servants. Emile drew nearer.

"You surely will not desert us now?" he said in a low voice.

"Please don't," she said vaguely. "I'm so worried," and, pushing quickly past him, she hurriedly rejoined the two women.

They were superintending the erection of a long tent or marquee in the garden, hastily extemporized from the awnings of the veranda and other cloth. Mrs. Randolph explained that, although all danger was over, there was the possibility of the recurrence of lighter shocks during the day and night, and that they would all feel much more secure and comfortable to camp out for the next twenty-four hours in the open air.

"Only imagine you're picnicking, and you'll enjoy it as most people usually enjoy those horrid *al fresco* entertainments. I don't believe there's the slightest real necessity for it, but," she added in a lower voice, "the Irish and Chinese servants are so demoralized now, they wouldn't stay indoors with us. It's a common practice here, I believe, for a day or two after the shock, and it gives time to put things right again and clear up. The old, one-storied, Spanish houses with walls three feet thick, and built round a courtyard or *patio*, were much safer. It's only when the Americans try to improve upon the old order of things with their pinchbeck shams and stucco that Providence interferes like this to punish them."

It was the fact, however, that Rose was more impressed by what seemed to her the absolute indifference of Providence in the matter, and the cool resumption by Nature of her ordinary conditions. The sky above their heads was as rigidly blue as ever, and as smilingly monotonous; the distant prospect, with its clear, well-known silhouettes, had not changed; the crows swung on lazy, deliberate wings over the grain as before; and the trade-wind was again blowing in its quiet persistency. And yet she knew that something had happened that would never again make her enjoyment of the prospect the same — that nothing would ever be as it was yesterday. I think at first she referred only to the material and larger phenomena, and did not confound this revelation of the insecurity of the universe with her experience of man. Yet the fact also remained that to the conservative, correct, and, as she believed, secure condition to which she had been approximating, all her relations were rudely shaken and upset. It really seemed to this simple-minded young woman that the revolutionary disturbance of settled conditions might have as Providential an origin as the " Divine Right" of which she had heard so much.

CHAPTER IV.

In her desire to be alone and to evade the now significant attentions of Emile, she took advantage of the bustle that followed the hurried transfer of furniture and articles from the house to escape through the garden to the outlying fields. Striking into one of the dusty lanes that she remembered, she wandered on for half an hour until her progress and meditation were suddenly arrested. She had come upon a long chasm or crack in the soil, full twenty feet wide and as many in depth, crossing her path at right angles. She did not remember having seen it before; the track of wheels went up to its precipitous edge; she could see the track on the other side, but the hiatus remained, unbridged and uncovered. It was not there yesterday. She glanced right and left; the fissure seemed to extend, like a moat or ditch, from the distant road to the upland between her and the great wheat valley below, from which she was shut off. An odd sense of being in some way a prisoner confronted her. She drew back with an impatient start, and perhaps her first real sense of indignation. A voice behind her, which she at once recognized, scarcely restored her calmness.

"You can't get across there, miss."

She turned. It was the young inventor from the wheat ranch, on horseback and with a clean face. He had just ridden out of the grain on the same side of the chasm as herself.

"But you seem to have got over," she said bluntly.

"Yes, but it was further up the field. I reckoned that the split might be deeper but not so broad in the rock outcrop over there than in the adobe here. I found it so and jumped it."

He looked as if he might — alert, intelligent, and self-contained. He lingered a moment, and then continued : —

"I'm afraid you must have been badly shaken and a little frightened up there before the chimneys came down ? "

"No," she was glad to say briefly, and she believed truthfully, "I was n't frightened. I did n't even know it was an earthquake."

"Ah!" he reflected, "that was because you were a stranger. It's odd — they're all like that. I suppose it's because nobody really expects or believes in the unlooked-for thing, and yet that's the thing that always happens. And then, of course, that other affair, which really is serious, startled you the more."

She felt herself ridiculously and angrily blushing. "I don't know what you mean," she said icily. "What other affair?"

"Why, the well."

"The well?" she repeated vacantly.

"Yes; the artesian well has stopped. Did n't the major tell you?"

"No," said the girl. "He was away; I have n't seen him yet."

"Well, the flow of water has ceased completely. That's what I'm here for. The major sent for me, and I've been to examine it."

"And is that stoppage so very important?" she said dubiously.

It was his turn to look at her wonderingly.

"If it's *lost* entirely, it means ruin for the ranch," he said sharply. He wheeled his horse, nodded gravely, and trotted off.

Major Randolph's figure of the "life-blood of the ranch" flashed across her suddenly. She knew nothing of irrigation or the costly appliances by which the Californian agriculturist opposed the long summer droughts. She only vaguely guessed that the dreadful earthquake had struck at the prosperity of those people whom only a few hours ago she had been proud to call her friends. The underlying goodness of her nature was touched. Should she let a momentary fault — if it were not really, after all, only a misunderstanding — rise between her and them at such a moment? She turned and hurried quickly towards the house.

Hastening onward, she found time, however, to wonder also why these common men — she now included even the young inventor in that category — were all so rude and uncivil to *her!* She had never before been treated in this way; she had always been rather embarrassed by the admiring attentions of young men (clerks and collegians) in her Atlantic home, and of professional men (merchants and stockbrokers) in San Francisco. It was true that they were not as continually devoted to her and to the nice

art and etiquette of pleasing as Emile, —
they had other things to think about, being
in business and not being *gentlemen,* — but
then they were greatly superior to these
clowns, who took no notice of her, and rode
off without lingering or formal leave-taking
when their selfish affairs were concluded.
It must be the contact of the vulgar earth
— this wretched, cracking, material, and yet
ungovernable and lawless earth — that so
depraved them. She felt she would like to
say this to some one — not her father, for he
would n't listen to her, nor to the major,
who would laughingly argue with her, but
to Mrs. Randolph, who would understand
her, and perhaps say it some day in her own
sharp, sneering way to these very clowns.
With those gentle sentiments irradiating her
blue eyes, and putting a pink flush upon her
fair cheeks, Rose reached the garden with
the intention of rushing sympathetically into
Mrs. Randolph's arms. But it suddenly occurred to her that she would be obliged to
state how she became aware of this misfor-
tune, and with it came an instinctive aver-
sion to speak of her meeting with the inventor. She would wait until Mrs. Randolph
told her. But although that lady was en-

gaged in a low-voiced discussion in French with Emile and Adele, which instantly ceased at her approach, there was no allusion made to the new calamity. "You need not telegraph to your father," she said as Rose approached, "he has already telegraphed to you for news; as you were out, and the messenger was waiting an answer, we opened the dispatch, and sent one, telling him that you were all right, and that he need not hurry here on your account. So you are satisfied, I hope." A few hours ago this would have been true, and Rose would have probably seen in the action of her hostess only a flattering motherly supervision; there was, in fact, still a lingering trace of trust in her mind; yet she was conscious that she would have preferred to answer the dispatch herself, and to have let her father come. To a girl brought up with a belief in the right of individual independence of thought and action, there was something in Mrs. Randolph's practical ignoring of that right which startled her in spite of her new conservatism, while, as the daughter of a business man, her instincts revolted against Mrs. Randolph's unbusiness-like action with the telegram, however vulgar and unrefined she may have begun to consider a life of business. The result was a certain constraint and embarrassment in her manner, which, however, had the laudable effect of limiting Emile's attention to significant glances, and was no doubt variously interpreted by the others. But she satisfied her conscience by determining to make a confidence of her sympathy to the major on the first opportunity.

This she presently found when the others were preoccupied ; the major greeting her with a somewhat careworn face, but a voice whose habitual kindness was unchanged. When he had condoled with her on the terrifying phenomenon that had marred her visit to the ranch, — and she could not help impatiently noticing that he too seemed to have accepted his wife's theory that she had been half deliriously frightened, — he regretted that her father had not concluded to come down to the ranch, as his practical advice would have been invaluable in this emergency. She was about to eagerly explain why, when it occurred to her that Mrs. Randolph had only given him a suppressed version of the telegram, and that she would be betraying her, or again taking sides in this partisan divided home. With some hesitation she at last alluded to the accident to the artesian well. The major did not ask her how she had heard of it; it was a bad business, he thought, but it might not be a total loss. The water may have been only diverted by the shock and might be found again at the lower level, or in some lateral fissure. He had sent hurriedly for Tom Bent —- that clever young engineer at the wheat ranch, who was always studying up these things with his inventions — and that was his opinion. No, Tom was not a well-digger, but it was generally known that he had "located" one or two, and had long ago advised the tapping of that flow by a second boring, in case of just such an emergency. He was coming again to-morrow. By the way, he had asked how the young lady visitor was, and hoped she had not been alarmed by the earthquake!

Rose felt herself again blushing, and, what was more singular, with an unexpected and it seemed to her ridiculous pleasure, although outwardly she appeared to ignore the civility completely. And she had no intention of being so easily placated. If this young man thought by mere perfunctory civilities to her *host* to make up for his clownishness to *her*, he was mistaken. She would let him see it when he called to-morrow. She quickly turned the subject by assuring the major of her sympathy and her intention of sending for her father. For the rest of the afternoon and during their *al fresco* dinner she solved the difficulty of her strained relations with Mrs. Randolph and Emile by conversing chiefly with the major, tacitly avoiding, however, any allusion to this Mr. Bent. But Mrs. Randolph was less careful.

"You don't really mean to say, major," she began in her dryest, grittiest manner, "that instead of sending to San Francisco for some skilled master-mechanic, you are going to listen to the vagaries of a conceited, half-educated farm-laborer, and employ him? You might as well call in some of those wizards or water-witches at once." But the major, like many other well-managed husbands who are good-humoredly content to suffer in the sunshine of prosperity, had no idea of doing so in adversity, and the prospect of being obliged to go back to youthful struggles had recalled some of the independence of that period. He looked up quietly, and said : —

" If his conclusions are as clear and satis-
factory to-morrow as they were to-day, I shall
certainly try to secure his services."

" Then I can only say *I* would prefer the
water-witch. He at least would not represent a class of neighbors who have made
themselves systematically uncivil and disagreeable to us."

" I am afraid, Josephine, we have not
tried to make ourselves particularly agreeable to *them*," said the major.

" If that can only be done by admitting
their equality, I prefer they should remain
uncivil. Only let it be understood, major,
that if you choose to take this Tom-the-
ploughboy to mend your well, you will at
least keep him there while he is on the
property."

With what retort the major would have
kept up this conjugal discussion, already beginning to be awkward to the discreet visitor,
is not known, as it was suddenly stopped by
a bullet from the rosebud lips of the ingen-
uous Adele.

" Why, he's very handsome when his face
is clean, and his hands are small and not at
all hard. And he does n't talk the least bit
queer or common."

There was a dead silence. "And pray where did *you* see him, and what do you know about his hands?" asked Mrs. Randolph, in her most desiccated voice. "Or has the major already presented you to him? I should n't be surprised."

"No, but " — hesitated the young girl, with a certain mouse-like audacity, — "when you sent me to look after Miss Mallory, I came up to him just after he had spoken to her, and he stopped to ask me how we all were, and if Miss Mallory was really frightened by the earthquake, and he shook hands for good afternoon — that's all."

"And who taught you to converse with common strangers and shake hands with them?" continued Mrs. Randolph, with narrowing lips.

"Nobody, mamma; but I thought if Miss Mallory, who is a young lady, could speak to him, so could I, who am not out yet."

"We won't discuss this any further at present," said Mrs. Randolph, stiffly, as the major smiled grimly at Rose. "The earthquake seems to have shaken down in this house more than the chimneys."

It certainly had shaken all power of sleep from the eyes of Rose when the household at last dispersed to lie down in their clothes on the mattresses which had been arranged under the awnings. She was continually starting up from confused dreams of the ground shaking under her, or she seemed to be standing on the brink of some dreadful abyss like the great chasm on the grain-field, when it began to tremble and crumble beneath her feet. It was near morning when, unable to endure it any longer, she managed without disturbing the sleeping Adele, who occupied the same curtained recess with her, to slip out from the awning. Wrapped in a thick shawl, she made her way through the encompassing trees and bushes of the garden that had seemed to imprison and suffocate her, to the edge of the grain-field, where she could breathe the fresh air beneath an open, starlit sky. There was no moon and the darkness favored her; she had no fears that weighed against the horror of seclusion with her own fancies. Besides, they were camping *out* of the house, and if she chose to sit up or walk about, no one could think it strange. She wished her father were here that she might have some one of her own kin to talk to, yet she knew not what to say to him if he had come. She wanted somebody to sympathize with her feelings, — or rather, perhaps, some one to combat and even ridicule the uneasiness that had lately come over her She knew what her father would say, — "Do you want to go, or do you want to stay here? Do you like these people, or do you not?" She remembered the one or two glowing and enthusiastic accounts she had written him of her visit here, and felt herself blushing again. What would he think of Mrs. Randolph's opening and answering the telegram? Would n't he find out from the major if she had garbled the sense of his dispatch?

Away to the right, in the midst of the distant and invisible wheat-field, there was the same intermittent star, which like a living, breathing thing seemed to dilate in glowing respiration, as she had seen it the first night of her visit. Mr. Bent's forge! It must be nearly daylight now; the poor fellow had been up all night, or else was stealing this early march on the day. She recalled Adele's sudden eulogium of him. The first natural smile that had come to her lips since the earthquake broke up her nervous restraint, and sent her back more like her old self to her couch.

But she had not proceeded far towards the tent, when she heard the sound of low voices approaching her. It was the major and his wife, who, like herself, had evidently been unable to sleep, and were up betimes. A new instinct of secretiveness, which she felt was partly the effect of her artificial surrounding, checked her first natural instinct to call to them, and she drew back deeper in the shadow to let them pass. But to her great discomfiture the major in a conversational emphasis stopped directly in front of her.

"You are wrong, I tell you, a thousand times wrong. The girl is simply upset by this earthquake. It's a great pity her father did n't come instead of telegraphing. And by Jove, rather than hear any more of this, I 'll send for him myself," said the major, in an energetic but suppressed voice.

"And the girl won't thank you, and you 'll be a fool for your pains," returned Mrs. Randolph, with dry persistency.

"But according to your own ideas of propriety, Mallory ought to be the first one to be consulted — and by me, too."

"Not in this case. Of course, before any actual engagement is on, you can speak of Emile's attentions."

"But suppose Mallory has other views. Suppose he declines the honor. The man is no fool."

"Thank you. But for that very reason he must. Listen to me, major; if he does n't care to please his daughter for her own sake, he will have to do so for the sake of decency. Yes, I tell you, she has thoroughly compromised herself — quite enough, if it is ever known, to spoil any other engagement her father may make. Why, ask Adele! The day of the earthquake she *absolutely* had the audacity to send him out of the room upstairs into your study for her fan, and then follow him up there alone. The servants knew it. I knew it, for I was in her room at the time with Father Antonio. The earthquake made it plain to everybody. Decline it! No. Mr. Mallory will think twice about it before he does that. What 's that? Who 's there?"

There was a sudden rustle in the bushes like the passage of some frightened animal — and then all was still again.

CHAPTER·V.

THE sun, an hour high, but only just topping the greenish crests of the wheat, was streaming like the morning breeze through the open length of Tom Bent's workshed. An exaggerated and prolonged shadow of the young inventor himself at work beside his bench was stretching itself far into the broken-down ranks of stalks towards the invisible road, and falling at the very feet of Rose Mallory as she emerged from them.

She was very pale, very quiet, and very determined. The traveling mantle thrown over her shoulders was dusty, the ribbons that tied her hat under her round chin had become unloosed. She advanced, walking down the line of shadow directly towards him.

"I am afraid I will have to trouble you once more," she said with a faint smile, which did not, however, reach her perplexed eyes. "Could you give me any kind of a

conveyance that would take me to San José
at once ? "

The young man had started at the rustling
of her dress in the shavings, and turned
eagerly. The faintest indication of a loss
of interest was visible for an instant in his
face, but it quickly passed into a smile of
recognition. Yet she felt that he had neither noticed any change in her appearance,
nor experienced any wonder at seeing her
there at that hour.

" I did not take a buggy from the house,"
she went on quickly, " for I left early, and
did not want to disturb them. In fact, they
don't know that I am gone. I was worried
at not hearing news from my father in
San Francisco since the earthquake, and I
thought I would run down to San José to
inquire without putting them to any trouble.
Anything will do that you have ready, if I
can take it at once."

Still without exhibiting the least surprise,
Bent nodded affirmatively, put down his
tools, begged her to wait a moment, and ran
off in the direction of the cabin. As he disappeared behind the wheat, she lapsed quite
suddenly against the work bench, but recovered herself a moment later, leaning with

her back against it, her hands grasping it on either side, and her knit brows and determined little face turned towards the road. Then she stood erect again, shook the dust out of her skirts, lifted her veil, wiped her cheeks and brow with the corner of a small handkerchief, and began walking up and down the length of the shed as Bent reappeared.

He was accompanied by the man who had first led her through the wheat. He gazed upon her with apparently all the curiosity and concern that the other had lacked.

" You want to get to San José as quick as you can?" he said interrogatively.

" Yes," she said quickly, " if you can help me."

" You walked all the way from the major's here?" he continued, without taking his eyes from her face.

" Yes," she answered with an affectation of carelessness she had not shown to Bent. " But I started very early, it was cool and pleasant, and did n't seem far."

" I 'll put you down in San José inside the hour. You shall have my horse and trotting sulky, and I 'll drive you myself. Will that do?"

She looked at him wonderingly. She had not forgotten his previous restraint and gravity, but now his face seemed to have relaxed with some humorous satisfaction. She felt herself coloring slightly, but whether with shame or relief she could not tell.

" I shall be *so* much obliged to you," she replied hesitatingly, " and so will my father, I know."

" I reckon," said the man with the same look of amused conjecture ; then, with a quick, assuring nod, he turned away, and dived into the wheat again.

" You 're all right now, Miss Mallory," said Bent, complacently. " Dawson will fix it. He 's got a good horse, and he 's a good driver, too." He paused, and then added pleasantly, " I suppose they 're all well up at the house ? "

It was so evident that his remark carried no personal meaning to herself that she was obliged to answer carelessly, " Oh, yes."

" I suppose you see a good deal of Miss Randolph — Miss Adele, I think you call her ? " he remarked tentatively, and with a certain boyish enthusiasm, which she had never conceived possible to his nature.

" Yes," she replied a little dryly, " she is

the only young lady there." She stopped, remembering Adele's naïve description of the man before her, and said abruptly, "You know her, then?"

"A little," replied the young man, modestly. "I see her pretty often when I am passing the upper end of the ranch. She's very well brought up, and her manners are very refined — don't you think so? — and yet she's just as simple and natural as a country girl. There's a great deal in education after all, isn't there?" he went on confidentially, "and although" — he lowered his voice and looked cautiously around him — "I believe that some of us here don't fancy her mother much, there's no doubt that Mrs. Randolph knows how to bring up her children. Some people think that kind of education is all artificial, and don't believe in it, but *I* do!"

With the consciousness that she was running away from these people and the shameful disclosure she had heard last night — with the recollection of Adele's scandalous interpretation of her most innocent actions and her sudden and complete revulsion against all that she had previously admired in that household, to hear this man who had seemed to her a living protest against their ideas and principles, now expressing them and holding them up for emulation, almost took her breath away.

" I suppose that means you intend to fix Major Randolph's well for him ? " she said dryly.

" Yes," he returned without noticing her manner ; " and I think I can find that water again. I 've been studying it up all night, and do you know what I 'm going to do ? I am going to make the earthquake that lost it help me to find it again." He paused, and looked at her with a smile and a return of his former enthusiasm. " Do you remember the crack in the adobe field that stopped you yesterday ? "

" Yes," said the girl, with a slight shiver.

" I told you then that the same crack was a split in the rock outcrop further up the plain, and was deeper. I am satisfied now, from what I have seen, that it is really a rupture of the whole strata all the way down. That 's the one weak point that the imprisoned water is sure to find, and that 's where the borer will tap it — in the new well that the earthquake itself has sunk."

It seemed to her now that she understood

his explanation perfectly, and she wondered
the more that he had been so mistaken in
his estimate of Adele. She turned away a
little impatiently and looked anxiously towards the point where Dawson had disappeared. Bent followed her eyes.

"He'll be here in a moment, Miss Mallory. He has to drive slowly through the
grain, but I hear the wheels." He stopped,
and his voice took up its previous note of
boyish hesitation. "By the way — I'll —
I'll be going up to the Rancho this afternoon to see the major. Have you any message for Mrs. Randolph — or for — for Miss
Adele?"

"No" — said Rose, hesitatingly, "and —
and" —

"I see," interrupted Bent, carelessly.
"You don't want anything said about your
coming here. I won't."

It struck her that he seemed to have no
ulterior meaning in the suggestion. But
before she could make any reply, Dawson
reappeared, driving a handsome mare harnessed to a light, spider-like vehicle. He
had also assumed, evidently in great haste, a
black frock coat buttoned over his waistcoat-
less and cravatless shirt, and a tall black hat

that already seemed to be cracking in the sunlight. He drove up, at once assisted her to the narrow perch beside him, and with a nod to Bent drove off. His breathless expedition relieved the leave-taking of these young people of any ceremony.

"I suppose," said Mr. Dawson, giving a half glance over his shoulder as they struck into the dusty highway, — "I suppose you don't care to see anybody before you get to San José?"

"No-o-o," said Rose, timidly.

"And I reckon you would n't mind my racin' a bit if anybody kem up?"

"No."

"The mare 's sort o' fastidious about takin' anybody's dust."

"Is she?" said Rose, with a faint smile.

"Awful," responded her companion; "and the queerest thing of all is, she can't bear to have any one behind her, either."

He leaned forward with his expression of humorous enjoyment of some latent joke and did something with the reins — Rose never could clearly understand what, though it seemed to her that he simply lifted them with ostentatious lightness; but the mare suddenly seemed to *lengthen* herself and lose

her height, and the stalks of wheat on either
side of the dusty track began to melt into
each other, and then slipped like a flash
into one long, continuous, shimmering green
hedge. So perfect was the mare's action
that the girl was scarcely conscious of any
increased effort ; so harmonious the whole
movement that the light skeleton wagon
seemed only a prolonged process of that long,
slim body and free, collarless neck, both
straight as the thin shafts on each side and
straighter than the delicate ribbon-like traces
which, in what seemed a mere affectation of
conscious power, hung at times almost limp
between the whiffle-tree and the narrow breast
band which was all that confined the animal's powerful fore-quarters. So superb
was the reach of its long easy stride that
Rose could scarcely see any undulations in
the brown shining back on which she could
have placed her foot, nor felt the soft beat
of the delicate hoofs that took the dust so
firmly and yet so lightly.

The rapidity of motion which kept them
both with heads bent forward and seemed to
force back any utterance that rose to their
lips spared Rose the obligation of conversation, and her companion was equally reti-

cent. But it was evident to her that he half suspected she was running away from the Randolphs, and that she wished to avoid the embarrassment of being overtaken even in persuasive pursuit. It was not possible that he knew the cause of her flight, and yet she could not account for his evident desire to befriend her, nor, above all, for his apparently humorous enjoyment of the situation. Had he taken it gravely, she might have been tempted to partly confide in him and ask his advice. Was she doing right, after all? Ought she not to have stayed long enough to speak her mind to Mrs. Randolph and demand to be sent home? No! She had not only shrunk from repeating the infamous slander she had overheard, but she had a terrible fear that if she had done so, Mrs. Randolph was capable of denying it, or even charging her of being still under the influence of the earthquake shock and of walking in her sleep. No! She could not trust her — she could trust no one there. Had not even the major listened to those infamous lies? Had she not seen that he was helpless in the hands of this cabal in his own household? — a cabal that she herself had thoughtlessly joined against him.

They had reached the first slight ascent. Her companion drew out his watch, looked at it with satisfaction, and changed the position of his hands on the reins. Without being able to detect the difference, she felt they were slackening speed. She turned inquiringly towards him; he nodded his head, with a half smile and a gesture to her to look ahead. The spires of San José were already faintly uplifting from the distant fringe of oaks.

So soon! In fifteen minutes she would be there — and *then!* She remembered suddenly she had not yet determined what to do. Should she go on at once to San Francisco, or telegraph to her father and await him at San José? In either case a new fear of the precipitancy of her action and the inadequacy of her reasons had sprung up in her mind. Would her father understand her? Would he underrate the cause and be mortified at the insult she had given the family of his old friend, or, more dreadful still, would he exaggerate her wrongs and seek a personal quarrel with the major. He was a man of quick temper, and had the Western ideas of redress. Perhaps even now she was precipitating a duel between them. Her cheeks grew wan again, her breath came quickly, tears gathered in her eyes. Oh, she was a dreadful girl, she knew it; she was an utterly miserable one, and she knew that too!

The reins were tightened. The pace lessened and at last fell to a walk. Conscious of her telltale eyes and troubled face, she dared not turn to her companion to ask him why, but glanced across the fields.

"When you first came I did n't get to know your name, Miss Mallory, but I reckon I know your father."

Her father! What made him say that? She wanted to speak, but she felt she could not. In another moment, if he went on, she must do *something* — she would cry!

"I reckon you 'll be wanting to go to the hotel first, anyway?"

There! — she knew it! He *would* keep on! And now she had burst into tears.

The mare was still walking slowly; the man was lazily bending forward over the shafts as if nothing had occurred. Then suddenly, illogically, and without a moment's warning, the pride that had sustained her crumbled and became as the dust of the road.

She burst out and told him — this stranger! — this man she had disliked! — all and *everything*. How she had felt, how she had been deceived, and what she had overheard!

"I thought as much," said her companion, quietly, "and that's why I sent for your father."

"You sent for my father! — when? — where?" echoed Rose, in astonishment.

"Yesterday. He was to come to-day, and if we don't find him at the hotel it will be because he has already started to come here by the upper and longer road. But you leave it to *me*, and don't you say anything to him of this now. If he's at the hotel, I'll say I drove you down there to show off the mare. *Sabe?* If he isn't, I'll leave you there and come back here to find him. I've got something to tell him that will set *you* all right." He smiled grimly, lifted the reins, the mare started forward again, and the vehicle and its occupants disappeared in a vanishing dust cloud.

CHAPTER VI.

IT was nearly noon when Mr. Dawson finished rubbing down his sweating mare in the little stable shed among the wheat. He had left Rose at the hotel, for they found Mr. Mallory had previously started by a circuitous route for the wheat ranch. He had resumed not only his working clothes but his working expression. He was now superintending the unloading of a wain of stores and implements when the light carryall of the Randolphs rolled into the field. It contained only Mrs. Randolph and the driver. A slight look of intelligence passed between the latter and the nearest one of Dawson's companions, succeeded, however, by a dull look of stupid vacancy on the faces of all the others, including Dawson. Mrs. Randolph noticed it, and was forewarned. She reflected that no human beings ever looked *naturally* as stupid as that and were able to work. She smiled sarcastically, and then began with dry distinctness and narrowing lips.

" Miss Mallory, a young lady visiting us, went out for an early walk this morning and has not returned. It is possible she may have lost her way among your wheat. Have you seen anything of her? "

Dawson raised his eyes from his work and glanced slowly around at his companions, as if taking the heavy sense of the assembly. One or two shook their heads mechanically, and returned to their suspended labor. He said, coolly : —

" Nobody here seems to."

She felt that they were lying. She was only a woman against five men. She was only a petty domestic tyrant; she might have been a larger one. But she had all the courage of that possibility.

" Major Randolph and my son are away," she went on, drawing herself erect. " But I know that the major will pay liberally if these men will search the field, besides making it all right with your — *employers* — for the loss of time."

Dawson uttered a single word in a low voice to the man nearest him, who apparently communicated it to the others, for the four men stopped unloading, and moved away one after the other — even the driver joining in the exodus. Mrs. Randolph smiled sarcastically; it was plain that these people, with all their boasted independence, were quite amenable to pecuniary considerations. Nevertheless, as Dawson remained looking quietly at her, she said : —

" Then I suppose they 've concluded to go and see ? "

" No ; I 've sent them away so that they could n't *hear.*"

" Hear what ? "

" What I 've got to say to you."

She looked at him suddenly. Then she said, with a disdainful glance around her : " I see I am helpless here, and — thanks to your trickery — alone. Have a care, sir ; I warn you that you will have to answer to Major Randolph for any insolence."

"I reckon you won't tell Major Randolph what I have to say to you," he returned coolly.

Her lips were nearly a grayish hue, but she said scornfully : " And why not ? Do you know who you are talking to ? "

The man came lazily forward to the carry-all, carelessly brushed aside the slack reins, and resting his elbows on the horse's back, laid his chin on his hands, as he looked up in the woman's face.

"Yes; *I* know who I'm talking to," he said coolly. "But as the major don't, I reckon you won't tell him."

"Stand away from that horse!" she said, her whole face taking the grayish color of her lips, but her black eyes growing smaller and brighter. "Hand me those reins, and let me pass! What *canaille* are you to stop me?"

"I thought so," returned the man, without altering his position; "you don't know *me*. You never saw *me* before. Well, I'm Jim Dawson, the nephew of L'Hommadieu, *your old master!*"

She gripped the iron rail of the seat as if to leap from it, but checked herself suddenly and leaned back, with a set smile on her mouth that seemed stamped there. It was remarkable that with that smile she flung away her old affectation of superciliousness for an older and ruder audacity, and that not only the expression, but the type of her face appeared to have changed.

"I don't say," continued the man quietly, "that he didn't *marry* you before he died. But you know as well as I do that the laws of his State didn't recognize the marriage of a master with his octoroon slave! And you know as well as I do that even if he had freed you, he could n't change your blood. Why, if I 'd been willing to stay at Avoyelles to be a nigger-driver like him, the plantation of ' de Fontanges ' — whose name you have taken — would have been left to me. If *you* had stayed there, you might have been my property instead of *your* owning a square man like Randolph. You did n't think of that when you came here, did you? " he said composedly.

" *Oh, mon Dieu !* " she said, dropping rapidly into a different accent, with her white teeth and fixed mirthless smile, " so it is a claim for *property*, eh? You 're wanting money — you? *Très bien*, you forget we are in California, where one does not own a slave. And you have a fine story there, my poor friend. Very pretty, but very hard to prove, *m'sieu*. And these peasants are in it, eh, working it on shares like the farm, eh ? "

" Well," said Dawson, slightly changing his position, and passing his hand over the horse's neck with a half-wearied contempt, " one of these men is from Plaquemine, and the other from Coupée. They know all the l'Hommadieus' history. And they know a streak of the tar brush when they see it. They took your measure when they came here last year, and sized you up fairly. So had I, for the matter of that, when I *first* saw you. And we compared notes. But the major is a square man, for all he is your husband, and we reckoned he had a big enough contract on his hands to take care of you and l'Hommadieu's half-breeds, and so " — he tossed the reins contemptuously aside — " we kept this to ourselves."

" And now you want — what — eh ? "

" We want an end to this foolery," he broke out roughly, stepping back from the vehicle, and facing her suddenly, with his first angry gesture. " We want an end to these airs and grimaces, and all this dandy nigger business; we want an end to this ' cake - walking ' through the wheat, and flouting of the honest labor of your betters. We want you and your ' de Fontanges ' to climb down. And we want an end to this roping-in of white folks to suit your little game ; we want an end to your trying to mix your nigger blood with any one here, and we intend to stop it. We draw the line at the major."

Lashed as she had been by those words

apparently out of all semblance of her former social arrogance, a lower and more stub-
born resistance seemed to have sprung up in
her, as she sat sideways, watching him with
her set smile and contracting eyes.

"Ah," she said dryly, "so *she is here.* I
thought so. Which of you is it, eh? It's
a good spec — Mallory's a rich man. She's
not particular."

The man had stopped as if listening, his
head turned towards the road. Then he
turned carelessly, and facing her again,
waved his hand with a gesture of tired dis-
missal, and said, "Go! You'll find your
driver over there by the tool-shed. He has
heard nothing yet — but I've given you fair
warning. Go!"

He walked slowly back towards the shed,
as the woman, snatching up the reins, drove
violently off in the direction where the men
had disappeared. But she turned aside,
ignoring her waiting driver in her wild and
reckless abandonment of all her old conventional attitudes, and lashing her horse forward with the same set smile on her face, the
same odd relaxation of figure, and the same
squaring of her elbows.

Avoiding the main road, she pushed into

a narrow track that intersected another nearer the scene of the accident to Rose's buggy three weeks before. She had nearly passed it when she was hailed by a strange voice, and looking up, perceived a horseman floundering in the mazes of the wheat to one side of the track. Whatever mean thought of her past life she was flying from, whatever mean purpose she was flying to, she pulled up suddenly, and as suddenly resumed her erect, aggressive stiffness. The stranger was a middle-aged man; in dress and appearance a dweller of cities. He lifted his hat as he perceived the occupant of the wagon to be a lady.

"I beg your pardon, but I fear I've lost my way in trying to make a short cut to the Excelsior Company's Ranch."

"You are in it now," said Mrs. Randolph, quickly.

"Thank you, but where can I find the farmhouse?"

"There is none," she returned, with her old superciliousness, "unless you choose to give that name to the shanties and sheds where the laborers and servants live, near the road."

The stranger looked puzzled. "I'm looking for a Mr. Dawson," he said reflectively, " but I may have made some mistake. Do you know Major Randolph's house hereabouts ? "

" I do. I am Mrs. Randolph," she said stiffly.

The stranger's brow cleared, and he smiled pleasantly. " Then this is a fortunate meeting," he said, raising his hat again as he reined in his horse beside the wagon, " for I am Mr. Mallory, and I was looking forward to the pleasure of presenting myself to you an hour or two later. The fact is, an old acquaintance, Mr. Dawson, telegraphed me yesterday to meet him here on urgent business, and I felt obliged to go there first."

Mrs. Randolph's eyes sparkled with a sudden gratified intelligence, but her manner seemed rather to increase than abate its grim precision.

" Our meeting this morning, Mr. Mallory, is both fortunate and unfortunate, for I regret to say that your daughter, who has not been quite herself since the earthquake, was missing early this morning and has not yet been found, though we have searched everywhere. Understand me," she said, as the stranger started, " I have no fear for her *personal* safety, I am only concerned for any *indiscretion* that she may commit in the presence of these strangers whose company she would seem to prefer to ours."

" But I don't understand you, madam," said Mallory, sternly; " you are speaking of my daughter, and " —

" Excuse me, Mr. Mallory," said Mrs. Randolph, lifting her hand with her driest deprecation and her most desiccating smile, " I 'm not passing judgment or criticism. I am of a foreign race, and consequently do not understand the freedom of American young ladies, and their familiarity with the opposite sex. I make no charges, I only wish to assure you that she will no doubt be found in the company and under the protection of her own countrymen. There is," she added with ironical distinctness, " a young mechanic, or field hand, or ' quack well-doctor,' whom she seems to admire, and with whom she appears to be on equal terms."

Mallory regarded her for a moment fixedly, and then his sternness relaxed to a mischievously complacent smile. " That must be young Bent, of whom I 've heard," he said with unabated cheerfulness. " And I don't know but what she may be with him, after all. For now I think of it, a chuckle-headed fellow, of whom a moment ago I inquired the way to your house, told me I 'd better ask the young man and young woman who were 'philandering through the wheat' yonder. Suppose we look for them. From what I 've heard of Bent he 's too much wrapped up in his inventions for flirtation, but it would be a good joke to stumble upon them."

Mrs. Randolph's eyes sparkled with a mingling of gratified malice and undisguised contempt for the fatuous father beside her. But before she could accept or decline the challenge, it had become useless. A murmur of youthful voices struck her ear, and she suddenly stood upright and transfixed in the carriage. For lounging down slowly towards them out of the dim green aisles of the arbored wheat, lost in themselves and the shimmering veil of their seclusion, came the engineer, Thomas Bent, and on his arm, gazing ingenuously into his face, the figure of Adele, — her own perfect daughter.

"I don't think, my dear," said Mr. Mallory, as the anxious Rose flew into his arms on his return to San José, a few hours later, " that it will be necessary for you to go back again to Major Randolph's before we leave. I have said 'Good-by' for you and thanked them, and your trunks are packed and will be sent here. The fact is, my dear, you see this affair of the earthquake and the disaster to the artesian well have upset all their arrangements, and I am afraid that my little girl would be only in their way just now."

" And you have seen Mr. Dawson — and you know why he sent for you?" asked the young girl, with nervous eagerness.

" Ah, yes," said Mr. Mallory thoughtfully, " *that* was really important. You see, my child," he continued, taking her hand in one of his own and patting the back of it gently with the other, " we think, Dawson and I, of taking over the major's ranch and incorporating it with the Excelsior in one, to be worked on shares like the Excelsior; and as Mrs. Randolph is very anxious to return to the Atlantic States with her children, it is quite possible. Mrs. Randolph, as you have possibly noticed," Mr. Mallory went on, still patting his daughter's hand, " does not feel entirely at home here, and will consequently leave the major free to rearrange, by himself, the ranch on the new basis. In fact, as the change must be made before the crops come in, she talks of going next week. But if you like the place, Rose, I 've no doubt the major and Dawson will always find room for you and me when we run down there for a little fresh air."

" And did you have all that in your mind, papa, when you came down here, and was that what you and Mr. Dawson wanted to talk about? " said the astonished Rose.

" Mainly, my dear, mainly. You see I 'm a capitalist now, and the real value of capital is to know how and when to apply it to certain conditions."

" And this Mr. — Mr. Bent — do you think — he will go on and find the water, papa?" said Rose, hesitatingly.

" Ah! Bent — Tom Bent — oh, yes," said Mallory, with great heartiness. " Capital fellow, Bent! and mighty ingenious! Glad you met him! Well," thoughtfully but still heartily, " he may not find it exactly where he expected, but he 'll find it or something better. We can't part with him, and he has promised Dawson to stay. We 'll utilize *him*, you may be sure."

It would seem that they did, and from certain interviews and conversations that took place between Mr. Bent and Miss Mallory on a later visit, it would also appear that her father had exercised a discreet reticence in regard to a certain experiment of the young inventor, of which he had been an accidental witness.

A MÆCENAS OF THE PACIFIC SLOPE.

CHAPTER I.

As Mr. Robert Rushbrook, known to an imaginative press as the "Mæcenas of the Pacific Slope," drove up to his country seat, equally referred to as a "palatial villa," he cast a quick but practical look at the pillared pretensions of that enormous shell of wood and paint and plaster. The statement, also a reportorial one, that its site, the Cañon of Los Osos, "some three years ago was disturbed only by the passing tread of bear and wild-cat," had lost some of its freshness as a picturesque apology, and already successive improvements on the original building seemingly cast the older part of the structure back to a hoary antiquity. To many it stood as a symbol of everything Robert Rushbrook did or had done — an improvement of all previous performances; it was like his own life — an exciting though irritating state of transition to something better. Yet the visible architectural result, as here shown, was scarcely harmonious; indeed, some of his friends — and Mæcenas had many — professed to classify the various improvements by the successive fortunate ventures in their owner's financial career, which had led to new additions, under the names of "The Comstock Lode Period," "The Union Pacific Renaissance," "The Great Wheat Corner," and "Water Front Gable Style," a humorous trifling that did not, however, prevent a few who were artists from accepting Mæcenas's liberal compensation for their services in giving shape to those ideas.

Relinquishing to a groom his fast-trotting team, the second relay in his two hours' drive from San Francisco, he leaped to the ground to meet the architect, already awaiting his orders in the courtyard. With his eyes still fixed upon the irregular building before him, he mingled his greeting and his directions.

"Look here, Barker, we'll have a wing thrown out here, and a hundred-foot ballroom. Something to hold a crowd; something that can be used for music — *sabe?* — a concert, or a show."

"Have you thought of any style, Mr. Rushbrook?" suggested the architect.

"No," said Rushbrook; "I've been thinking of the time — thirty days, and everything to be in. You'll stop to dinner. I'll have you sit near Jack Somers. You can talk style to him. Say I told you."

"You wish it completed in thirty days?" repeated the architect, dubiously.

"Well, I shouldn't mind if it were less. You can begin at once. There's a telegraph in the house. Patrick will take any message, and you can send up to San Francisco and fix things before dinner."

Before the man could reply, Rushbrook was already giving a hurried interview to the gardener and others on his way to the front porch. In another moment he had entered his own hall, — a wonderful temple of white and silver plaster, formal, yet friable like the sugared erection of a wedding cake, — where his major-domo awaited him.

"Well, who's here?" asked Rushbrook, still advancing towards his apartments.

"Dinner is set for thirty, sir," said the functionary, keeping step demurely with his

master, " but Mr. Appleby takes ten over to
San Mateo, and some may sleep there. The
char-à-banc is still out and five saddle-horses,
to a picnic in Green Cañon, and I can't positively say, but I should think you might
count on seeing about forty-five guests before
you go to town to-morrow. The opera troupe
seem to have not exactly understood the invitation, sir."

" How ?   I gave it myself."

" The chorus and supernumeraries thought
themselves invited too, sir, and have come, I
believe, sir.   At least Signora Pegrelli and
Madame Denise said so, and that they would
speak to you about it, but that meantime I
could put them up anywhere."

" And you made no distinction, of course ? "

" No, sir, I put them in the corresponding
rooms opposite, sir.   I don't think the prima
donnas like it."

" Ah ! "

" Yes, sir."

Whatever was in their minds, the two
men never changed their steady, practical
gravity of manner.   The major-domo's appeared to be a subdued imitation of his master's, worn, as he might have worn his
master's clothes, had he accepted, or Mr.

Rushbrook permitted, such a degradation. By this time they had reached the door of Mr. Rushbrook's room, and the man paused. " I did n't include some guests of Mr. Leyton's, sir, that he brought over here to show around the place, but he told me to tell you he would take them away again, or leave them, as you liked. They 're some Eastern strangers stopping with him."

" All right," said Rushbrook, quietly, as he entered his own apartment. It was decorated as garishly as the hall, as staring and vivid in color, but wholesomely new and clean for all its paint, veneering, and plaster. It was filled with heterogeneous splendor — all new and well kept, yet with so much of the attitude of the show-room still lingering about it that one almost expected to see the various articles of furniture ticketed with their prices. A luxurious bed, with satin hangings and Indian carved posts, standing ostentatiously in a corner, kept up this resemblance, for in a curtained recess stood a worn camp bedstead, Rushbrook's real couch, Spartan in its simplicity.

Mr. Rushbrook drew his watch from his pocket, and deliberately divested himself of his boots, coat, waistcoat, and cravat. Then rolling himself in a fleecy, blanket-like rug with something of the habitual dexterity of a frontiersman, he threw himself on his couch, closed his eyes, and went instantly to sleep. Lying there, he appeared to be a man comfortably middle-aged, with thick iron-gray hair that might have curled had he encouraged such inclination; a skin roughened and darkened by external hardships and exposure, but free from taint of inner vice or excess, and indistinctive features redeemed by a singularly handsome mouth. As the lower part of the face was partly hidden by a dense but closely-cropped beard, it is probable that the delicate outlines of his lips had gained something from their framing.

He slept, through what seemed to be the unnatural stillness of the large house, — a quiet that might have come from the lingering influence of the still virgin solitude around it, as if Nature had forgotten the intrusion, or were stealthily retaking her own; and later, through the rattle of returning wheels or the sound of voices, which were, however, promptly absorbed in that deep and masterful silence which was the unabdicating genius of the cañon. For it was remarkable that even the various artists, musicians, orators, and poets whom Mæcenas had gathered in his cool business fashion under that roof, all seemed to become, by contrast with surrounding Nature, as new and artificial as the house, and as powerless to assert themselves against its influence.

He was still sleeping when James reentered the room, but awoke promptly at the sound of his voice. In a few moments he had rearranged his scarcely disordered toilette, and stepped out refreshed and observant into the hall. The guests were still absent from that part of the building, and he walked leisurely past the carelessly opened doors of the rooms they had left. Everywhere he met the same glaring ornamentation and color, the same garishness of treatment, the same inharmonious extravagance of furniture, and everywhere the same troubled acceptance of it by the inmates, or the same sense of temporary and restricted tenancy. Dresses were hung over cheval glasses ; clothes piled up on chairs to avoid the use of doubtful and over ornamented wardrobes, and in some cases more practical guests had apparently encamped in a corner

of their apartment. A gentleman from Siskyou — sole proprietor of a mill patent now
being considered by Mæcenas — had confined himself to a rocking-chair and clothes-
horse as being trustworthy and familiar; a
bolder spirit from Yreka — in treaty for capital to start an independent journal devoted
to Mæcenas's interests — had got a good deal
out of, and indeed all he had *into*, a Louis
XVI. *armoire ;* while a young painter from
Sacramento had simply retired into his adjoining bath-room, leaving the glories of his
bedroom untarnished. Suddenly he paused.

He had turned into a smaller passage in
order to make a shorter cut through one of
the deserted suites of apartments that should
bring him to that part of the building where
he designed to make his projected improvement, when his feet were arrested on the
threshold of a sitting - room. Although it
contained the same decoration and furniture
as the other rooms, it looked totally different! It was tasteful, luxurious, comfortable, and habitable. The furniture seemed
to have fallen into harmonious position;
even the staring decorations of the walls and
ceiling were toned down by sprays of laurel
and red-stained *manzanito* boughs with their

berries, apparently fresh plucked from the near cañon. But he was more unexpectedly impressed to see that the room was at that moment occupied by a tall, handsome girl, who had paused to take breath, with her hand still on the heavy centre-table she was moving. Standing there, graceful, glowing, and animated, she looked the living genius of the recreated apartment.

CHAPTER II.

MR. RUSHBROOK glanced rapidly at his unknown guest. "Excuse me," he said, with respectful business brevity, "but I thought every one was out," and he stepped backward quickly.

"I've only just come," she said without embarrassment, "and would you mind, as you *are* here, giving me a lift with this table?"

"Certainly," replied Rushbrook, and under the young girl's direction the millionaire moved the table to one side.

During the operation he was trying to determine which of his unrecognized guests the fair occupant was. Possibly one of the Leyton party, that James had spoken of as impending.

"Then you have changed all the furniture, and put up these things?" he asked, pointing to the laurel.

"Yes, the room was really something *too* awful. It looks better now, don't you think?"

"A hundred per cent.," said Rushbrook, promptly. "Look here, I'll tell you what you've done. You've set the furniture *to work !* It was simply lying still — with no return to anybody on the investment."

The young girl opened her gray eyes at this, and then smiled. The intruder seemed to be characteristic of California. As for Rushbrook, he regretted that he did not know her better ; he would at once have asked her to rearrange all the rooms, and have managed in some way liberally to reward her for it. A girl like that had no nonsense about her.

"Yes," she said, "I wonder Mr. Rushbrook don't look at it in that way. It is a shame that all these pretty things — and you know they are really good and valuable — should n't show what they are. But I suppose everybody here accepts the fact that this man simply buys them because they are valuable, and nobody interferes, and is content to humor him, laugh at him, and feel superior. It don't strike me as quite fair, does it you ? "

Rushbrook was pleased. Without the vanity that would be either annoyed at this revelation of his reputation, or gratified at her defense of it, he was simply glad to discover that she had not recognized him as her host, and could continue the conversation unreservedly. "Have you seen the ladies' boudoir?" he asked. "You know, the room fitted with knick-knacks and pretty things — some of 'em bought from old collections in Europe, by fellows who knew what they were ; but perhaps," he added, looking into her eyes for the first time, "did n't know exactly what ladies cared for."

"I merely glanced in there when I first came, for there was such a queer lot of women — I 'm told he is n't very particular in that way — that I did n't stay."

"And you did n't think *they* might be just as valuable and good as some of the furniture, if they could have been pulled around and put into shape, or set in a corner, eh?"

The young girl smiled ; she thought her fellow-guest rather amusing, none the less so, perhaps, for catching up her own ideas, but nevertheless she slightly shrugged her shoulders with that hopeless skepticism which women reserve for their own sex. "Some of them looked as if they had been pulled around, as you say, and had n't been improved by it."

"There's no one there now," said Rushbrook, with practical directness; "come and
take a look at it." She complied without
hesitation, walking by his side, tall, easy,
and self - possessed, apparently accepting
without self-consciousness his half paternal,
half comrade - like informality. The boudoir was a large room, repeating on a bigger
scale the incongruousness and ill - fitting
splendor of the others. When she had of
her own accord recognized and pointed out
the more admirable articles, he said, gravely
looking at his watch, "We've just about
seven minutes yet; if you'd like to pull
and haul these things around, I'll help
you."

The young girl smiled. "I'm quite content with what I've done in my own room,
where I have no one's taste to consult but
my own. I hardly know how Mr. Rushbrook, or his lady friends, might like my
operating here." Then recognizing with
feminine tact the snub that might seem
implied in her refusal, she said quickly,
"Tell me something about our host — but
first look! isn't that pretty?"

She had stopped before the window that
looked upon the dim blue abyss of the cañon,

and was leaning out to gaze upon it. Rush-brook joined her.

"There is n't much to be changed down *there*, is there?" he said, half interroga-tively.

"No, not unless Mr. Rushbrook took it into his head to roof it in, and somebody was ready with a contract to do it. But what do you know of him? Remember, I 'm quite a stranger here."

"You came with Charley Leyton?"

"With *Mrs.* Leyton's party," said the young girl, with a half-smiling emphasis. "But it seems that we don't know whether Mr. Rushbrook wants us here or not, till he comes. And the drollest thing about it is that they 're all so perfectly frank in saying so."

"Charley and he are old friends, and you 'll do well to trust to their judgment."

This was hardly the kind of response that the handsome and clever society girl before him had been in the habit of receiving, but it amused her. Her fellow-guest was de-cidedly original. But he had n't told her about Rushbrook, and it struck her that his opinion would be independent, at least. She reminded him of it.

"Look here," said Rushbrook, "you'll meet a man here to-night — or he'll be sure to meet *you* — who'll tell you all about Rushbrook. He's a smart chap, knows everybody and talks well. His name is Jack Somers; he is a great ladies' man. He can talk to you about these sort of things, too," — indicating the furniture with a half tolerant, half contemptuous gesture, that struck her as inconsistent with what seemed to be his previous interest, — "just as well as he can talk of people. Been in Europe, too."

The young girl's eye brightened with a quick vivacity at the name, but a moment after became reflective and slightly embarrassed. "I know him — I met him at Mr. Leyton's. He has already talked of Mr. Rushbrook, but," she added, avoiding any conclusion, with a pretty pout, "I'd like to have the opinion of others. Yours, now, I fancy would be quite independent."

"You stick to what Jack Somers has said, good or bad, and you won't be far wrong," he said assuringly. He stopped; his quick ear had heard approaching voices; he returned to her and held out his hand. As it seemed to her that in California everybody shook hands with everybody else on the slightest occasions, sometimes to save further conversation, she gave him her own. He shook it, less forcibly than she had feared, and abruptly left her. For a moment she was piqued at this superior and somewhat brusque way of ignoring her request, but reflecting that it might be the awkwardness of an untrained man, she dismissed it from her mind. The voices of her friends in the already resounding passages also recalled her to the fact that she had been wandering about the house with a stranger, and she rejoined them a little self-consciously.

"Well, my dear," said Mrs. Leyton, gayly, "it seems we are to stay. Leyton says Rushbrook won't hear of our going."

"Does that mean that your husband takes the whole opera troupe over to your house in exchange?"

"Don't be satirical, but congratulate yourself on your opportunity of seeing an awfully funny gathering. I wouldn't have you miss it for the world. It's the most characteristic thing out."

"Characteristic of what?"

"Of Rushbrook, of course. Nobody else would conceive of getting together such a lot of queer people."

" But don't it strike you that we 're a part of the lot ? "

" Perhaps," returned the lively Mrs. Leyton. " No doubt that 's the reason why Jack Somers is coming over, and is so anxious that *you* should stay. I can't imagine why else he should rave about Miss Grace Nevil as he does. Come, Grace, no New York or Philadelphia airs, here ! Consider your uncle's interests with this capitalist, to say nothing of ours. Because you 're a millionaire and have been accustomed to riches from your birth, don't turn up your nose at our unpampered appetites. Besides, Jack Somers is Rushbrook's particular friend, and he may think your criticisms unkind."

" But *is* Mr. Somers such a great friend of Mr. Rushbrook's ? " asked Grace Nevil.

" Why, of course. Rushbrook consults him about all these things ; gives him *carte blanche* to invite whom he likes and order what he likes, and trusts his taste and judgment implicitly."

" Then this gathering is Mr. Somers's selection ? "

" How preposterous you are, Grace. Of course not. Only Somers's *idea* of what is pleasing to Rushbrook, gotten up with a taste and discretion all his own. You know Somers is a gentleman, educated at West Point — traveled all over Europe — you might have met him there ; and Rushbrook — well, you have only to see him to know what *he* is. Don't you understand ?"

A slight seriousness; the same shadow that once before darkened the girl's charming face gave way to a mischievous knitting of her brows as she said naïvely, " No."

CHAPTER III.

GRACE NEVIL had quite recovered her equanimity when the indispensable Mr. Somers, handsome, well-bred, and self-restrained, approached her later in the crowded drawing-room. Blended with his subdued personal admiration was a certain ostentation of respect — as of a tribute to a distinguished guest — that struck her. " I am to have the pleasure of taking you in, Miss Nevil," he said. " It 's my one compensation for the dreadful responsibility just thrust upon me. Our host has been suddenly called away, and I am left to take his place."

Miss Nevil was slightly startled. Nevertheless, she smiled graciously. "From what I hear this is no new function of yours ; that is, if there really *is* a Mr. Rushbrook. I am inclined to think him a myth."

" You make me wish he were," retorted Somers, gallantly ; " but as I could n't reign at all, except in his stead, I shall look to you to lend your rightful grace to my borrowed dignity."

The more general announcement to the company was received with a few perfidious regrets from the more polite, but with only amused surprise by the majority. Indeed, many considered it "characteristic" — "so like Bob Rushbrook," and a few enthusiastic friends looked upon it as a crowning and intentional stroke of humor. It remained, however, for the gentleman from Siskyou to give the incident a subtlety that struck Miss Nevil's fancy. "It reminds me," he said in her hearing, "of ole Kernel Frisbee, of Robertson County, one of the purlitest men I ever struck. When he knew a feller was very dry, he'd jest set the decanter afore him, and managed to be called outer the room on bus'ness. Now, Bob Rushbrook's about as white a man as that. He's jest the feller, who, knowing you and me might feel kinder restrained about indulging our appetites afore him, kinder drops out easy, and leaves us alone." And she was impressed by an instinct that the speaker really felt the delicacy he spoke of, and that it left no sense of inferiority behind.

The dinner, served in a large, brilliantly-lit saloon, that in floral decoration and gilded columns suggested an ingenious blending of a steamboat *table d'hôte* and "harvest home," was perfect in its *cuisine*, even if somewhat extravagant in its proportions.

"I should be glad to receive the salary that Rushbrook pays his *chef*, and still happier to know how to earn it as fairly," said Somers to his fair companion.

"But is his skill entirely appreciated here?" she asked.

"Perfectly," responded Somers. "Our friend from Siskyou over there appreciates that *pâté* which he cannot name as well as I do. Rushbrook himself is the only exception, yet I fancy that even *his* simplicity and regularity in feeding is as much a matter of business with him as any defect in his earlier education. In his eyes, his *chef's* greatest qualification is his promptness and fertility. Have you noticed that ornament before you?" pointing to an elaborate confection. "It bears your initials, you see. It was conceived and executed since you arrived — rather, I should say, since it was known that you would honor us with your company. The greatest difficulty encountered was to find out what your initials were."

"And I suppose," mischievously added

the young girl to her acknowledgments, "that the same fertile mind which conceived the design eventually provided the initials?"

"That is our secret," responded Somers, with affected gravity.

The wines were of characteristic expensiveness, and provoked the same general comment. Rushbrook seldom drank wine; Somers had selected it. But the barbaric opulence of the entertainment culminated in the Californian fruits, piled in pyramids on silver dishes, gorgeous and unreal in their size and painted beauty, and the two Divas smiled over a basket of grapes and peaches as outrageous in dimensions and glaring color as any pasteboard banquet at which they had professionally assisted. As the courses succeeded each other, under the exaltation of wine, conversation became more general as regarded participation, but more local and private as regarded the subject, until Miss Nevil could no longer follow it. The interests of that one, the hopes of another, the claims of a third, in affairs that were otherwise uninteresting, were all discussed with singular youthfulness of trust that to her alone seemed remarkable. Not

that she lacked entertainment from the conversation of her clever companion, whose
confidences and criticisms were very pleasant to her ; but she had a gentlewoman's instinct that he talked to her too much, and
more than was consistent with his duties as
the general host. She looked around the table
for her singular acquaintance of an hour before, but she had not seen him since. She
would have spoken about him to Somers, but
she had an instinctive idea that the latter
would be antipathetic, in spite of the stranger's flattering commendation. So she found
herself again following Somers's cynical but
good - humored description of the various
guests, and, I fear, seeing with his eyes,
listening with his ears, and occasionally
participating in his superior attitude. The
" fearful joy " she had found in the novelty
of the situation and the originality of the
actors seemed now quite right from this critical point of view. So she learned how the
guest with the long hair was an unknown
painter, to whom Rushbrook had given a
commission for three hundred yards of
painted canvas, to be cut up and framed as
occasion and space required, in Rushbrook's
new hotel in San Francisco ; how the gray-

bearded foreigner near him was an accomplished bibliophile who was furnishing Mr.
Rushbrook's library from spoils of foreign
collections, and had suffered unheard - of
agonies from the millionaire's insisting upon
a handsome uniform binding that should de-
prive certain precious but musty tomes of
their crumbling, worm-eaten coverings; how
the very gentle, clerical-looking stranger,
mildest of a noisy, disputing crowd at the
other table, was a notorious duelist and dead
shot; how the only gentleman at the table
who retained a flannel shirt and high boots
was not a late-coming mountaineer, but a
well-known English baronet on his travels;
how the man who told a somewhat florid
and emphatic anecdote was a popular Eastern clergyman; how the one querulous, discontented face in a laughing group was the
famous humorist who had just convulsed it;
and how a pale, handsome young fellow, who
ate and drank sparingly and disregarded the
coquettish advances of the prettiest *Diva*
with the cold abstraction of a student, was a
notorious *roué* and gambler.   But there was
a sudden and unlooked-for change of criticism and critic.

The festivity had reached that stage when

the guests were more or less accessible to emotion, and more or less touched by the astounding fact that every one was enjoying himself. This phenomenon, which is apt to burst into song or dance among other races, is constrained to voice itself in an Anglo-Saxon gathering by some explanation, apology, or moral — known as an after-dinner speech. Thus it was that the gentleman from Siskyou, who had been from time to time casting glances at Somers and his fair companion at the head of the table, now rose to his feet, albeit unsteadily, pushed back his chair, and began : —

" 'Pears to me, ladies and gentlemen, and feller pardners, that on an occasion like this, suthin' oughter be said of the man who got it up — whose money paid for it, and who ain't here to speak for himself, except by deputy. Yet you all know that 's Bob Rushbrook's style — he ain't here, because he 's full of some other plan or improvements — and it 's like him to start suthin' of this kind, give it its aim and purpose, and then stand aside to let somebody else run it for him. There ain't no man livin' ez hez, so to speak, more fast horses ready saddled for riding, and more fast men ready spurred to ride

'em, — whether to win his races or run his
errands.   There ain't no man livin' ez knows
better how to make other men's games his,
or his game seem to be other men's.   And
from Jack Somers smilin' over there, ez
knows where to get the best wine that Bob
pays for, and knows how to run this yer
show for Bob, at Bob's expense — we're all
contented.   Ladies and gentlemen, we're
all contented.   We stand, so to speak, on
the cards he's dealt us.   What may be his
little game, it ain't for us to say; but whatever it is, *we're in it.*   Gentlemen and ladies, we'll drink Bob's health!"

There was a somewhat sensational pause,
followed by good-natured laughter and ap-
plause, in which Somers joined; yet not
without a certain constraint that did not
escape the quick sympathy of the shocked
and unsmiling Miss Nevil.   It was with a
feeling of relief that she caught the chaper-
oning eye of Mrs. Leyton, who was entreat-
ing her in the usual mysterious signal to the
other ladies to rise and follow her.   When
she reached the drawing-room, a little behind
the others, she was somewhat surprised to
observe that the stranger whom she had
missed during the evening was approaching
her with Mrs. Leyton.

" Mr. Rushbrook returned sooner than he expected, but unfortunately, as he always retires early, he has only time to say 'good-night' to you before he goes."

For an instant Grace Nevil was more angry than disconcerted. Then came the conviction that she was stupid not to have suspected the truth before. Who else would that brusque stranger develop into but this rude host? She bowed formally.

Mr. Rushbrook looked at her with the faintest smile on his handsome mouth. " Well, Miss Nevil, I hope Jack Somers satisfied your curiosity? "

With a sudden recollection of the Siskyou gentleman's speech, and a swift suspicion that in some way she had been made use of with the others by this forceful-looking man before her, she answered pertly: —

" Yes; but there was a speech by a gentleman from Siskyou that struck me as being nearer to the purpose."

" That 's so, — I heard it as I came in," said Mr. Rushbrook, calmly. " I don't know but you 're right."

CHAPTER IV.

Six months had passed. The Villa of Mæcenas was closed at Los Osos Cañon, and the southwest trade-winds were slanting the rains of the wet season against its shut windows and barred doors. Within that hollow, deserted shell, its aspect — save for a single exception — was unchanged; the furniture and decorations preserved their eternal youth undimmed by time; the rigidly-arranged rooms, now closed to life and light, developed more than ever their resemblance to a furniture warehouse. The single exception was the room which Grace Nevil had rearranged for herself; and that, oddly enough, was stripped and bare — even to its paper and mouldings.

In other respects, the sealed treasures of Rushbrook's villa, far from provoking any sentimentality, seemed only to give truth to the current rumor that it was merely waiting to be transformed into a gorgeous watering-place hotel under Rushbrook's direction;

that, with its new ball-room changed into an elaborate dining-hall, it would undergo still further improvement, the inevitable end and object of all Rushbrook's enterprise; and that its former proprietor had already begun another villa whose magnificence should eclipse the last. There certainly appeared to be no limit to the millionaire's success in all that he personally undertook, or in his fortunate complicity with the enterprise and invention of others. His name was associated with the oldest and safest schemes, as well as the newest and boldest — with an equal guarantee of security. A few, it was true, looked doubtingly upon this "one man power," but could not refute the fact that others had largely benefited by association with him, and that he shared his profits with a royal hand. Some objected on higher grounds to his brutalizing the influence of wealth by his material and extravagantly practical processes, instead of the gentler suggestions of education and personal example, and were impelled to point out the fact that he and his patronage were vulgar. It was felt, however, by those who received his benefits, that a proper sense of this inferiority was all that ethics demanded of them.

One could still accept Rushbrook's barbaric
gifts by humorously recognizing the fact
that he did n't know any better, and that it
pleased him, as long as they resented any
higher pretensions.

The rain-beaten windows of Rushbrook's
town house, however, were cheerfully lit that
December evening. Mr. Rushbrook seldom
dined alone ; in fact, it was popularly alleged
that very often the unfinished business of the
day was concluded over his bountiful and
perfect board. He was dressing as James
entered the room.

"Mr. Leyton is in your study, sir ; he will
stay to dinner."

"All right."

"I think, sir," added James, with respectful suggestiveness, "he wants to talk. At
least, sir, he asked me if you would likely
come downstairs before your company arrived."

"Ah ! Well, tell the others I 'm dining
on *business*, and set dinner for two in the
blue room."

"Yes, sir."

Meanwhile, Mr. Leyton — a man of Rushbrook's age, but not so fresh and vigorous-
looking — had thrown himself in a chair

beside the study fire, after a glance around
the handsome and familiar room. For the
house had belonged to a brother millionaire;
it had changed hands with certain shares of
" Water Front," — as some of Rushbrook's
dealings had the true barbaric absence of
money detail, — and was elegantly and taste-
fully furnished. The cuckoo had, however,
already laid a few characteristic eggs in this
adopted nest, and a white marble statue of
a nude and ill-fed Virtue, sent over by Rushbrook's Paris agent, and unpacked that morning, stood in one corner, and materially
brought down the temperature. A Japanese
praying-throne of pure ivory, and, above it,
a few yards of improper, colored exposure
by an old master, equalized each other.

"And what is all this affair about the
dinner?" suddenly asked a tartly-pitched
female voice with a foreign accent.

Mr. Leyton turned quickly, and was just
conscious of a faint shriek, the rustle of a
skirt, and the swift vanishing of a woman's
figure from the doorway. Mr. Leyton turned
red. Rushbrook lived *en garçon*, with feminine possibilities; Leyton was a married
man and a deacon. The incident which, to
a man of the world, would have brought

only a smile, fired the inexperienced Leyton with those exaggerated ideas and intense credulity regarding vice common to some very good men. He walked on tip-toe to the door, and peered into the passage. At that moment Rushbrook entered from the opposite door of the room.

"Well," said Rushbrook, with his usual practical directness, "what do you think of her?"

Leyton, still flushed, and with eyebrows slightly knit, said, awkwardly, that he had scarcely seen her.

"She cost me already ten thousand dollars, and I suppose I'll have to eventually fix up a separate room for her somewhere," continued Rushbrook.

"I should certainly advise it," said Leyton, quickly, "for really, Rushbrook, you know that something is due to the respectable people who come here, and any of them are likely to see" —

"Ah!" interrupted Rushbrook, seriously, "you think she hasn't got on clothes enough. Why, look here, old man — she's one of the Virtues, and that's the rig in which they always travel. She's a 'Temperance' or a 'Charity' or a 'Resignation,' or something of that kind. You 'll find her name there in French somewhere at the foot of the marble."

Leyton saw his mistake, but felt — as others sometimes felt — a doubt whether this smileless man was not inwardly laughing at him. He replied, with a keen, rapid glance at his host : —

" I was referring to some woman who stood in that doorway just now, and addressed me rather familiarly, thinking it was you."

" Oh, the Signora," said Rushbrook, with undisturbed directness; " well, you saw her at Los Osos last summer. Likely she *did* think you were me."

The cool ignoring of any ulterior thought in Leyton's objection forced the guest to be equally practical in his reply.

" Yes, but the fact is that Miss Nevil had talked of coming here with me this evening to see you on her own affairs, and it would n't have been exactly the thing for her to meet that woman."

" She would n't," said Rushbrook, promptly; " nor would *you*, if you had gone into the parlor as Miss Nevil would have done. But look here! If that 's the reason why you did n't bring her, send for her at once; my coachman can take a card from you; the brougham's all ready to fetch her, and there you are. She'll see only you and me." He was already moving towards the bell, when Leyton stopped him.

"No matter now. I can tell you her business, I fancy; and in fact, I came here to speak of it, quite independently of her."

"That won't do, Leyton," interrupted Rushbrook, with crisp decision. "One or the other interview is unnecessary; it wastes time, and is n't business. Better have her present, even if she don't say a word."

"Yes, but not in this matter," responded Leyton; "it's about Somers. You know he's been very attentive to her ever since her uncle left her here to recruit her health, and I think she fancies him. Well, although she's independent and her own mistress, as you know, Mrs. Leyton and I are somewhat responsible for her acquaintance with Somers, — and for that matter so are you; and as my wife thinks it means a marriage, we ought to know something more positive about Somers's prospects. Now, all we really know is that he's a great friend of yours; that you trust a good deal to him;

that he manages your social affairs; that you treat him as a son or nephew, and it's generally believed that he's as good as provided for by you — eh? Did you speak?"

" No," said Rushbrook, quietly regarding the statue as if taking its measurement for a suitable apartment for it. " Go on."

" Well," said Leyton, a little impatiently, " that's the belief everybody has, and you've not contradicted it. And on that we've taken the responsibility of not interfering with Somers's attentions."

" Well? " said Rushbrook, interrogatively.

" Well," replied Leyton, emphatically, " you see I must ask you positively if you *have* done anything, or are you going to do anything for him? "

" Well," replied Rushbrook, with exasperating coolness, " what do you call this marriage? "

" I don't understand you," said Leyton.

" Look here, Leyton," said Rushbrook, suddenly and abruptly facing him; " Jack Somers has brains, knowledge of society, tact, accomplishments, and good looks: that's *his* capital as much as mine is money. I employ him: that's his advertisement, recommendation, and credit. Now, on the strength of this, as you say, Miss Nevil is willing to invest in him; I don't see what more can be done."

"But if her uncle don't think it enough?"

"She 's independent, and has money for both."

"But if she thinks she 's been deceived, and changes her mind?"

"Leyton, you don't know Miss Nevil. Whatever that girl undertakes she 's weighed fully, and goes through with. If she 's trusted him enough to marry him, money won't stop her; if she thinks she 's been deceived, *you 'll* never know it."

The enthusiasm and conviction were so unlike Rushbrook's usual cynical toleration of the sex that Leyton stared at him.

"That 's odd," he returned. "That 's what she says of you."

"Of *me;* you mean Somers?"

"No, of *you*. Come, Rushbrook, don't pretend you don't know that Miss Nevil is a great partisan of yours, swears by you, says you 're misunderstood by people, and, what 's infernally odd in a woman who don't belong to the class you fancy, don't talk of your habits. That 's why she wants to consult you about Somers, I suppose, and that 's why, knowing you might influence her, I came here first to warn you."

"And I 've told you that whatever I might say or do would n't influence her. So we 'll drop the subject."

"Not yet; for you 're bound to see Miss Nevil sooner or later. Now, if she knows that you 've done nothing for this man, your friend and her lover, won't she be justified in thinking that you would have a reason for it?"

"Yes. I should give it."

"What reason?"

"That I knew she 'd be more contented to have him speculate with *her* money than mine."

"Then you think that he is n't a business man?"

"I think that she thinks so, or she would n't marry him; it 's part of the attraction. But come, James has been for five minutes discreetly waiting outside the door to tell us dinner is ready, and the coast clear of all other company. But look here," he said, suddenly stopping, with his arm in Leyton's, "you 're through your talk, I suppose; perhaps you 'd rather we 'd dine with the Signora and the others than alone?"

For an instant Leyton thrilled with the fascination of what he firmly believed was a guilty temptation. Rushbrook, perceiving his hesitation, added : —

" By the way, Somers is of the party, and one or two others you know."

Mr. Leyton opened his eyes widely at this; either the temptation had passed, or the idea of being seen in doubtful company by a younger man was distasteful, for he hurriedly disclaimed any preference. " But," he added with half-significant politeness, " perhaps I 'm keeping *you* from them ? "

" It makes not the slightest difference to me," calmly returned Rushbrook, with such evident truthfulness that Leyton was both convinced and chagrined.

Preceded by the grave and ubiquitous James, they crossed the large hall, and entered through a smaller passage a charming apartment hung with blue damask, which might have been a boudoir, study, or small reception-room, yet had the air of never having been anything continuously. It would seem that Rushbrook's habit of " camping out " in different parts of his mansion obtained here as at Los Osos, and with the exception of a small closet which contained his Spartan bed, the rooms were used separately or in suites, as occasion or his friends required. It is recorded that an Eastern guest, newly arrived with letters to Rushbrook, after a tedious journey, expressed himself pleased with this same blue room, in which he had sumptuously dined with his host, and subsequently fell asleep in his chair. Without disturbing his guest, Rushbrook had the table removed, a bed, washstand, and bureau brought in, the sleeping man delicately laid upon the former, and left to awaken to an Arabian night's realization of his wish.

CHAPTER V.

JAMES had barely disposed of his master
and Mr. Leyton, and left them to the minis-
trations of two of his underlings, before he
was confronted with one of those difficult
problems that it was part of his functions to
solve. The porter informed him that a
young lady had just driven up in a carriage
ostensibly to see Mr. Rushbrook, and James,
descending to the outer vestibule, found himself face to face with Miss Grace Nevil.
Happily, that young lady, with her usual
tact, spared him some embarrassment.

"Oh! James," she said sweetly, "do you
think that I could see Mr. Rushbrook for a
few moments *if I waited for the opportunity?* You understand, I don't wish to
disturb him or his company by being regularly announced."

The young girl's practical intelligence appeared to increase the usual respect which
James had always shown her. "I understand, miss." He thought for a moment,

and said: " Would you mind, then, following me where you could wait quietly and
alone?" As she quickly assented, he preceded her up the staircase, past the study
and drawing-room, which he did not enter,
and stopped before a small door at the end
of the passage. Then, handing her a key
which he took from his pocket, he said:
" This is the only room in the house that is
strictly reserved for Mr. Rushbrook, and
even he rarely uses it. You can wait here
without anybody knowing it until I can com-
municate with him and bring you to his
study unobserved. And," he hesitated, " if
you would n't mind locking the door when
you are in, miss, you would be more secure,
and I will knock when I come for you."

Grace Nevil smiled at the man's prudence,
and entered the room. But to her great
surprise, she had scarcely shut the door when
she was instantly struck with a singular
memory which the apartment recalled. It
was exactly like the room she had altered in
Rushbrook's villa at Los Osos! More than
that, on close examination it proved to be
the very same furniture, arranged as she
remembered to have arranged it, even to the
flowers and grasses, now, alas! faded and

withered on the walls. There could be no mistake. There was the open ebony *escritoire* with the satin blotter open, and its leaves still bearing the marks of her own handwriting. So complete to her mind was the idea of her own tenancy in this bachelor's mansion, that she looked around with a half indignant alarm for the photograph or portrait of herself that might further indicate it. But there was no other exposition. The only thing that had been added was a gilt legend on the satin case of the blotter, — " Los Osos, August 20, 186–," the day she had occupied the room.

She was pleased, astonished, but more than all, disturbed. The only man who might claim a right to this figurative possession of her tastes and habits was the one whom she had quietly, reflectively, and understandingly half accepted as her lover, and on whose account she had come to consult Rushbrook. But Somers was not a sentimentalist; in fact, as a young girl, forced by her independent position to somewhat critically scrutinize masculine weaknesses, this had always been a point in his favor; yet even if he had joined with his friend Rushbrook to perpetuate the memory of their first acquaintanceship, his taste merely would not have selected a *chambre de garçon* in Mr. Rushbrook's home for its exhibition. Her conception of the opposite characters of the two men was singularly distinct and real, and this momentary confusion of them was disagreeable to her woman's sense. But at this moment James came to release her and conduct her to Rushbrook's study, where he would join her at once. Everything had been arranged as she had wished.

Even a more practical man than Rushbrook might have lingered over the picture of the tall, graceful figure of Miss Nevil, quietly enthroned in a large armchair by the fire, her scarlet, satin-lined cloak thrown over its back, and her chin resting on her hand. But the millionaire walked directly towards her with his usual frankness of conscious but restrained power, and she felt, as she always did, perfectly at her ease in his presence. Even as she took his outstretched hand, its straightforward grasp seemed to endow her with its own confidence.

" You 'll excuse my coming here so abruptly," she smiled, " but I wanted to get before Mr. Leyton, who, I believe, wishes to see you on the same business as myself."

" He is here already, and dining with me,"
said Rushbrook.

" Ah! does he know I am here? " asked
the girl, quietly.

" No; as he said you had thought of coming with him and did n't, I presumed you
did n't care to have him know you had come
alone."

" Not exactly that, Mr. Rushbrook," she
said, fixing her beautiful eyes on him in
bright and trustful confidence, " but I happen to have a fuller knowledge of this business than he has, and yet, as it is not altogether my own secret, I was not permitted
to divulge it to him. Nor would I tell it to
you, only I cannot bear that you should
think that I had anything to do with this
wretched inquisition into Mr. Somers's prospects. Knowing as well as you do how perfectly independent I am, you would think
it strange, would n't you? But you would
think it still more surprising when you found
out that I and my uncle already know how
liberally and generously you had provided
for Mr. Somers in the future."

" How I had provided for Mr. Somers in
the future? " repeated Mr. Rushbrook, looking at the fire, " eh? "

"Yes," said the young girl, indifferently, "how you were to put him in to succeed you in the Water Front Trust, and all that. He told it to me and my uncle at the outset of our acquaintance, confidentially, of course, and I dare say with an honorable delicacy that was like him, but — I suppose now you will think me foolish — all the while I 'd rather he had not."

"You 'd rather he had not," repeated Mr. Rushbrook, slowly.

"Yes," continued Grace, leaning forward with her rounded elbows on her knees, and her slim, arched feet on the fender. "Now you are going to laugh at me, Mr. Rushbrook, but all this seemed to me to spoil any spontaneous feeling I might have towards him, and limit my independence in a thing that should be a matter of free will alone. It seemed too much like a business proposition! There, my kind friend!" she added, looking up and trying to read his face with a half girlish pout, followed, however, by a maturer sigh, "I 'm bothering you with a woman's foolishness instead of talking business. And " — another sigh — " I suppose it *is* business for my uncle, who has, it seems, bought into this Trust on these possible contingencies, has, perhaps, been asking questions of Mr. Leyton. But I don't want you to think that I approve of them, or advise your answering them. But you are not listening."

" I had forgotten something," said Rushbrook, with an odd preoccupation. " Excuse me a moment — I will return at once."

He left the room quite as abstractedly, and when he reached the passage, he apparently could not remember what he had forgotten, as he walked deliberately to the end window, where, with his arms folded behind his back, he remained looking out into the street. A passer-by, glancing up, might have said he had seen the pale, stern ghost of Mr. Rushbrook, framed like a stony portrait in the window. But he presently turned away, and reëntered the room, going up to Grace, who was still sitting by the fire, in his usual strong and direct fashion.

" Well! Now let me see what you want. I think this would do."

He took a seat at his open desk, and rapidly wrote a few lines.

" There," he continued, " when you write to your uncle, inclose that."

Grace took it, and read : —

DEAR MISS NEVIL, — Pray assure your
uncle from me that I am quite ready to guarantee, in any form that he may require, the
undertaking represented to him by Mr. John
Somers. Yours very truly,

ROBERT RUSHBROOK.

A quick flush mounted to the young girl's
cheeks. " But this is a *security*, Mr. Rushbrook," she said proudly, handing him back
the paper, "and my uncle does not require
that. Nor shall I insult him or you by sending it."

"It is *business*, Miss Nevil," said Rushbrook, gravely. He stopped, and fixed his
eyes upon her animated face and sparkling
eyes. " You can send it to him or not, as
you like. But " — a rare smile came to his
handsome mouth — "as this is a letter to
you, you must not insult *me* by not accepting it."

Replying to his smile rather than the
words that accompanied it, Miss Nevil
smiled, too. Nevertheless, she was uneasy
and disturbed. The interview, whatever she
might have vaguely expected from it, had
resolved itself simply into a business in-
dorsement of her lover, which she had not

sought, and which gave her no satisfaction. Yet there was the same potent and indefinably protecting presence before her which she had sought, but whose omniscience and whose help she seemed to have lost the spell and courage to put to the test. He relieved her in his abrupt but not unkindly fashion. " Well, when is it to be?"

"It?"

" Your marriage."

"Oh, not for some time. There's no hurry."

It might have struck the practical Mr. Rushbrook that, even considered as a desirable business affair, the prospective completion of this contract provoked neither frank satisfaction nor conventional dissimulation on the part of the young lady, for he regarded her calm but slightly wearied expression fixedly. But he only said: " Then I shall say nothing of this interview to Mr. Leyton?"

" As you please. It really matters little. Indeed, I suppose I was rather foolish in coming at all, and wasting your valuable time for nothing."

She had risen, as if taking his last question in the significance of a parting suggestion, and was straightening her tall figure, preparatory to putting on her cloak. As she reached it, he stepped forward, and lifted it from the chair to assist her. The act was so unprecedented, as Mr. Rushbrook never indulged in those minor masculine courtesies, that she was momentarily as confused as a younger girl at the gallantry of a younger man. In their previous friendship he had seldom drawn near her except to shake her hand — a circumstance that had always recurred to her when his free and familiar life had been the subject of gossip. But she now had a more frightened consciousness that her nerves were strangely responding to his powerful propinquity, and she involuntarily contracted her pretty shoulders as he gently laid the cloak upon them. Yet even when the act was completed, she had a superstitious instinct that the significance of this rare courtesy was that it was final, and that he had helped her to interpose something that shut him out from her forever.

She was turning away with a heightened color, when the sound of light, hurried footsteps, and the rustle of a woman's dress was heard in the hall. A swift recollection of her companion's infelicitous reputation now returned to her, and Grace Nevil, with a slight stiffening of her whole frame, became coldly herself again. Mr. Rushbrook betrayed neither surprise nor agitation. Begging her to wait a moment until he could arrange for her to pass to her carriage unnoticed, he left the room.

Yet it seemed that the cause of the disturbance was unsuspected by Mr. Rushbrook. Mr. Leyton, although left to the consolation of cigars and liquors in the blue room, had become slightly weary of his companion's prolonged absence. Satisfied in his mind that Rushbrook had joined the gayer party, and that he was even now paying gallant court to the Signora, he became again curious and uneasy. At last the unmistakable sound of whispering voices in the passage got the better of his sense of courtesy as a guest, and he rose from his seat, and slightly opened the door. As he did so the figures of a man and woman, conversing in earnest whispers, passed the opening. The man's arm was round the woman's waist; the woman was — as he had suspected — the one who had stood in the doorway, the Signora — but — the man was *not* Rushbrook. Mr. Leyton drew back this time in unaffected horror. It was none other than Jack Somers!

Some warning instinct must at that moment have struck the woman, for with a stifled cry she disengaged herself from Somers's arm, and dashed rapidly down the hall. Somers, evidently unaware of the cause, stood irresolute for a moment, and then more silently but swiftly disappeared into a side corridor as if to intercept her. It was the rapid passage of the Signora that had attracted the attention of Grace and Rushbrook in the study, and it was the moment after it that Mr. Rushbrook left.

CHAPTER VI.

VAGUELY uneasy, and still perplexed with her previous agitation, as Mr. Rushbrook closed the door behind him, Grace, following some feminine instinct rather than any definite reason, walked to the door and placed her hand upon the lock to prevent any intrusion until he returned. Her caution seemed to be justified a moment later, for a heavier but stealthier footstep halted outside. The handle of the door was turned, but she resisted it with the fullest strength of her small hand until a voice, which startled her, called in a hurried whisper: —

"Open quick, 't is I."

She stepped back quickly, flung the door open, and beheld Somers on the threshold!

The astonishment, agitation, and above all, the awkward confusion of this usually self-possessed and ready man, was so unlike him, and withal so painful, that Grace hurried to put an end to it, and for an instant forgot her own surprise at seeing him. She smiled assuringly, and extended her hand.

" Grace — Miss Nevil — I beg your pardon — I did n't imagine " — he began with a forced laugh. " I mean, of course — I cannot — but " —. He stopped, and then assuming a peculiar expression, said: " But what are *you* doing here ? "

At any other moment the girl would have resented the tone, which was as new to her as his previous agitation, but in her present self-consciousness her situation seemed to require some explanation. " I came here," she said, " to see Mr. Rushbrook on business. Your business — *our* business," she added, with a charming smile, using for the first time the pronoun that seemed to indicate their unity and interest, and yet fully aware of a vague insincerity in doing so.

" Our *business?* " he repeated, ignoring her gentler meaning with a changed emphasis and a look of suspicion.

" Yes," said Grace, a little impatiently. " Mr. Leyton thought he ought to write to my uncle something positive as to your prospects with Mr. Rushbrook, and " —

" You came here to inquire ? " said the young man, sharply.

" I came here to stop any inquiry," said Grace, indignantly. " I came here to say *I*

was satisfied with what you had confided to
me of Mr. Rushbrook's generosity, and that
was enough ! "

" With what *I* had confided to you ? You
dared say that ? "

Grace stopped, and instantly faced him.
But any indignation she might have felt at
his speech and manner was swallowed up in
the revulsion and horror that overtook her
with the sudden revelation she saw in his
white and frightened face. Leyton's strange
inquiry, Rushbrook's cold composure and
scornful acceptance of her own credulous-
ness, came to her in a flash of shameful intelligence. Somers had lied ! The insufferable
meanness of it ! A lie, whose very useless-
ness and ignobility had defeated its purpose
— a lie that implied the basest suspicion of
her own independence and truthfulness —
such a lie now stood out as plainly before her
as his guilty face.

" Forgive my speaking so rudely," he said
with a forced smile and attempt to recover
his self-control, " but you have ruined me
unless you deny that I told you anything.
It was a joke — an extravagance that I had
forgotten ; at least, it was a confidence between you and me that you have foolishly

violated. Say that you misunderstood me —
that it was a fancy of your own. Say anything — he trusts you — he'll believe anything you say."

" He *has* believed me," said Grace, almost
fiercely, turning upon him with the paper
that Rushbrook had given her in her outstretched hand. " Read that!"

He read it. Had he blushed, had he stammered, had he even kept up his former frantic and pitiable attitude, she might at that
supreme moment have forgiven him. But to
her astonishment his face changed, his handsome brow cleared, his careless, happy smile
returned, his graceful confidence came back
— he stood before her the elegant, courtly,
and accomplished gentleman she had known.
He returned her the paper, and advancing
with extended hand, said triumphantly: —

" Superb! Splendid! No one but a
woman could think of that! And only one
woman achieve it. You have tricked the
great Rushbrook. You are indeed worthy
of being a financier's wife!"

" No," she said passionately, tearing up
the paper and throwing it at his feet; " not
as *you* understand it — and never *yours!*
You have debased and polluted everything

connected with it, as you would have debased and polluted *me*. Out of my presence that you are insulting — out of the room of the man whose magnanimity you cannot understand ! "

The destruction of the guarantee apparently stung him more than the words that accompanied it. He did not relapse again into his former shamefaced terror, but as a malignant glitter came into his eyes, he regained his coolness.

" It may not be so difficult for others to understand, Miss Nevil," he said, with polished insolence, " and as Bob Rushbrook's generosity to pretty women is already a matter of suspicion, perhaps you are wise to destroy that record of it."

" Coward ! " said Grace, " stand aside and let me pass ! " She swept by him to the door. But it opened upon Rushbrook's reentrance. He stood for an instant glancing at the pair, and then on the fragments of the paper that strewed the floor. Then, still holding the door in his hand, he said quietly : —

" One moment before you go, Miss Nevil. If this is the result of any misunderstanding as to the presence of another woman here, in company with Mr. Somers, it is only fair to him to say that that woman is here as a friend of *mine*, not of his, and I alone am responsible."

Grace halted, and turned the cold steel of her proud eyes on the two men. As they rested on Rushbrook they quivered slightly. "I can already bear witness," she said coldly, " to the generosity of Mr. Rushbrook in a matter which then touched me. But there certainly is no necessity for him to show it now in a matter in which I have not the slightest concern."

As she swept out of the room and was received in the respectable shadow of the waiting James, Rushbrook turned to Somers.

" And *I'm* afraid it won't do — for Leyton saw you," he said curtly. " Now, then, shut that door, for you and I, Jack Somers, have a word to say to each other."

What that word was, and how it was said and received, is not a part of this record. But it is told that it was the beginning of that mighty Iliad, still remembered of men, which shook the financial camps of San Francisco, and divided them into bitter contending parties. For when it became known the next day that Somers had suddenly abandoned Rushbrook, and carried over to a powerful foreign capitalist the secret methods, and even, it was believed, the *luck* of his late employer, it was certain that there would be war to the knife, and that it was no longer a struggle of rival enterprise, but of vindictive men.

CHAPTER VII

For a year the battle between the Somers faction and the giant but solitary Rushbrook raged fiercely, with varying success. I grieve to say that the *protégés* and parasites of Mæcenas deserted him in a body; nay, they openly alleged that it was the true artistic nature and refinement of Somers that had always attracted them, and that a man like Rushbrook, who bought pictures by the yard, — equally of the unknown struggling artist and the famous masters, — was no true patron of Art. Rushbrook made no attempt to recover his lost prestige, and once, when squeezed into a tight " corner," and forced to realize on his treasures, he put them up at auction and the people called them " daubs ; " their rage knew no bounds. It was then that an unfettered press discovered that Rushbrook never was a Mæcenas at all, grimly deprecated his assumption of that title, and even doubted if he were truly a millionaire. It was at this time that a few stood by him — notably, the mill inventor from Siskyou, grown plethoric with success, but eventually ground between the upper and nether millstone of the Somers and Rushbrook party. Miss Nevil had returned to the Atlantic States with Mrs. Leyton. While rumors had played freely with the relations of Somers and the Signora as the possible cause of the rupture between him and Rushbrook, no mention had ever been made of the name of Miss Nevil.

It was raining heavily one afternoon, when Mr. Rushbrook drove from his office to his San Francisco house. The fierce struggle in which he was engaged left him little time for hospitality, and for the last two weeks his house had been comparatively deserted. He passed through the empty rooms, changed in little except the absence of some valuable monstrosities which had gone to replenish his capital. When he reached his bedroom, he paused a moment at the open door.

" James ! "

" Yes, sir," said James, appearing out of the shadow.

" What are you waiting for ? "

" I thought you might be wanting something, sir."

" You were waiting there this morning; you were in the ante-room of my study while I was writing. You were outside the blue room while I sat at breakfast. You were at my elbow in the drawing-room late last night. Now, James," continued Mr. Rushbrook, with his usual grave directness, " I don't intend to commit suicide ; I can't afford it, so keep your time and your rest for yourself — you want it — that 's a good fellow."

" Yes, sir."

" James ! "

" Yes, sir."

Rushbrook extended his hand. There was that faint, rare smile on his handsome mouth, for which James would at any time have laid down his life. But he only silently grasped his master's hand, and the two men remained looking into each other's eyes without a word. Then Mr. Rushbrook entered his room, lay down, and went to sleep, and James vanished in the shadow.

At the end of an hour Mr. Rushbrook awoke refreshed, and even James, who came to call him, appeared to have brightened in the interval. " I have ordered a fire, sir, in the reserved room, the one fitted up from Los Osos, as your study has had no chance of being cleaned these two weeks. It will be a change for you, sir. I hope you'll excuse my not waking you to consult you about it."

Rushbrook remained so silent that James, fancying he had not heard him, was about to repeat himself when his master said quickly, " Very well, come for me there when dinner is ready," and entered the passage leading to the room. James did not follow him, and when Mr. Rushbrook, opening the door, started back with an exclamation, no one but the inmate heard the word that rose to his lips.

For there, seated before the glow of the blazing fire, was Miss Grace Nevil. She had evidently just arrived, for her mantle was barely loosened around her neck, and upon the fringe of brown hair between her bonnet and her broad, low forehead a few drops of rain still sparkled. As she lifted her long lashes quickly towards the door, it seemed as if they, too, had caught a little of that moisture. Rushbrook moved impatiently forward, and then stopped. Grace rose unhesitatingly to her feet, and met him half-way with frankly outstretched hands. " First of all," she said, with a half nervous laugh, "don't scold James; it's all my fault; I forbade him to announce me, lest you should drive me away, for I heard that during this excitement you came here for rest, and saw no one. Even the intrusion into this room is all my own. I confess now that I saw it the last night I was here; I was anxious to know if it was unchanged, and made James bring me here. I did not understand it then. I do now — and — thank you."

Her face must have shown that she was conscious that he was still holding her hand, for he suddenly released it. With a heightened color and a half girlish *naïveté*, that was the more charming for its contrast with her tall figure and air of thoroughbred repose, she turned back to her chair, and lightly motioned him to take the one before her. "I am here on *business;* otherwise I should not have dared to look in upon you at all."

She stopped, drew off her gloves with a provoking deliberation, which was none the less fascinating that it implied a demure consciousness of inducing some impatience in the breast of her companion, stretched them out carefully by the fingers, laid them down neatly on the table, placed her elbows on her knees, slightly clasped her hands together, and bending forward, lifted her honest, handsome eyes to the man before her.

" Mr. Rushbrook, I have got between four and five hundred thousand dollars that I have no use for; I can control securities which can be converted, if necessary, into a hundred thousand more in ten days. I am free and my own mistress. It is generally considered that I know what I am about — you admitted as much when I was your pupil. I have come here to place this sum in your hands, at your free disposal. You know why and for what purpose."

" But what do you know of my affairs ? " asked Rushbrook, quickly.

" Everything, and I know *you*, which is better. Call it an investment if you like — for I know you will succeed — and let me share your profits. Call it — if you please — restitution, for I am the miserable cause of your rupture with that man. Or call it revenge if you like," she said with a faint smile, "and let me fight at your side against our common enemy ! Please, Mr. Rushbrook, don't deny me this. I have come three thousand miles for it; I could have sent it to you — or written — but I feared you would not understand it. You are smiling — you will take it?"

" I cannot," said Rushbrook, gravely.

" Then you force me to go into the Stock Market myself, and fight for you, and, unaided by *your* genius, perhaps lose it without benefiting you."

Rushbrook did not reply.

" At least, then, tell me why you 'cannot.' "

Rushbrook rose, and looking into her face, said quietly with his old directness: —

" Because I love you, Miss Nevil."

A sudden instinct to rise and move away, a greater one to remain and hear him speak again, and a still greater one to keep back the blood that she felt was returning all too quickly to her cheek after the first shock, kept her silent. But she dropped her eyes.

" I loved you ever since I first saw you at Los Osos," he went on quickly; " I said to myself even then, that if there was a woman that would fill my life, and make me what she wished me to be, it was you. I even fancied that day that you understood me better than any woman, or even any man, that I had ever met before. I loved you through all that miserable business with that man, even when my failure to make you happy with another brought me no nearer to you. I have loved you always. I shall love you always. I love you more for this foolish kindness that brings *you* beneath my roof once more, and gives me a chance to speak my heart to you, if only once and for the last time, than all the fortune that you could put at my disposal. But I could not accept what you would offer me from any woman who was not my wife — and I could not marry any woman that did not love me. I am perhaps past the age when I could inspire a young girl's affection; but I have not reached the age when I would accept anything less." He stopped abruptly. Grace did not look up. There was a tear glistening upon her long eyelashes, albeit a faint smile played upon her lips.

"Do you call this business, Mr. Rushbrook?" she said softly.

"Business?"

"To assume a proposal declined before it has been offered."

"Grace — my darling — tell me — is it possible?"

It was too late for her to rise now, as his hands held both hers, and his handsome mouth was smiling level with her own. So it really seemed to a dispassionate spectator that it *was* possible, and befcre she had left the room, it even appeared to be the most probable thing in the world.

.   .   .   .

The union of Grace Nevil and Robert Rushbrook was recorded by local history as the crown to his victory over the Ring. But only he and his wife knew that it was the cause.

Works of Fiction.

A List of Novels and Stories, selected from the Publications of Messrs. Houghton, Mifflin and Company, Boston and New York.

Thomas Bailey Aldrich.
The Story of a Bad Boy. Illustrated. 12mo, $1.25.

Marjorie Daw and Other People. Short Stories. With Frontispiece. 12mo, $1.50.

Marjorie Daw and Other Stories. In Riverside Aldine Series. 16mo, $1.00.

These volumes are not identical in contents.

Prudence Palfrey. With Frontispiece. 12mo, $1.50; paper, 50 cents.

The Queen of Sheba. 12mo, $1.50; paper, 50 cents.

The Stillwater Tragedy. 12mo, $1.50.

Lucia True Ames.
Memoirs of a Millionaire. 16mo, $1.25.

Hans Christian Andersen.
Works. First Complete Edition in English. In ten uniform volumes, 12mo, each $1.00; the set, $10.00; half calf, $25.00.

The Improvisatore; or, Life in Italy.
The Two Baronesses.
O. T.; or, Life in Denmark.
Only a Fiddler.

In Spain and Portugal.
A Poet's Bazaar. A Picturesque Tour.
Pictures of Travel
The Story of my Life. With Portrait.
Wonder Stories told for Children. Illustrated.
Stories and Tales. Illustrated.

Jane G. Austin.

A Nameless Nobleman. 16mo, $1.25 ; paper, 50 cents.

The Desmond Hundred. 16mo, $1.00 ; paper, 50 cents.

Standish of Standish. 16mo, $1.25.

Doctor LeBaron and His Daughters. 16mo, $1.25.

Arlo Bates.

The Philistines. 12mo, $1.50.

It has many strong situations, much admirable dialogue, and we consider it decidedly the best thing Mr. Bates has yet done. — *New York Tribune.*

Patty's Perversities. 16mo, $1.00 ; paper, 50 cents.

The Pagans. 16mo, $1.00 ; paper, 50 cents.

Edward Bellamy.

Miss Ludington's Sister. 16mo, $1.25 ; paper, 50 cents.

Looking Backward: 2000–1887. 371st Thousand. 12mo, $1.00 ; paper, 50 cents.

Ein Rückblick (Looking Backward). Translated into German by Rabbi Solomon Schindler. 16mo, paper, 50 cents.

"Looking Backward" is a well-made book, but it is more — a glowing prophecy and a gospel of peace. He who reads it expecting merely to be entertained, must, we should think, find himself unexpectedly haunted by visions of a golden age wherein all the world unites to do the world's work like members of one family, where labor and living are provided for each man, where toil and leisure alternate in happy proportions, where want and therefore greed and jealousy are unknown, where the pleasures of this world are free to all, to cheer, but not to enslave. — *The Nation* (New York).

Mr. Bellamy's wonderful book. — EDWARD EVERETT HALE.

William Henry Bishop.

Detmold : A Romance. 18mo, $1.25.

The House of a Merchant Prince. 12mo, $1.50.

Choy Susan, and other Stories. 16mo, $1.25.

The Golden Justice. 16mo, $1.25 ; paper, 50 cents.

Mr. W. D. Howells, in *Harper's Monthly*, praises this volume highly, saying : "As a study of a prosperous western city, this picture of Keewaydin is unique in our literature." He adds that "it is full of traits of mastery which cannot leave any critic doubtful of Mr. Bishop's power."

Björnstjerne Björnson.

Novels. American Edition. Translated by Prof. R. B. Anderson. Including Synnöve Solbakken, Arne, The Bridal March, A Happy Boy, The Fisher Maiden, Captain Mansana, and Magnhild. Illustrated. In 3 volumes, 12mo, $4.50.

The Bridal March, and other Stories. Illustrated. 16mo, $1.00.

Captain Mansana, and other Stories. 16mo, $1.00.

Alice Brown.

Fools of Nature. 12mo, $1.50 ; paper, 50 cents.

Helen Dawes Brown.

Two College Girls. 12mo, $1.50 ; paper, 50 cents.

H. C. Bunner.

A Woman of Honor. 16mo, $1.25; paper, 50 cents.

Clara Louise Burnham.

Young Maids and Old. 12mo, $1.50; paper, 50 cents.
Next Door. 12mo, $1.50; paper, 50 cents.
Dearly Bought. New Edition. 16mo, $1.25.
No Gentlemen. New Edition. 16mo, $1.25.
A Sane Lunatic. New Edition. 16mo, $1.25.
The Mistress of Beech Knoll. 16mo, $1.25.

Edwin Lassetter Bynner.

Agnes Surriage. 12mo, $1.50; paper, 50 cents.

We congratulate the author on a well-earned success, and the reader on an unusual pleasure. — T. B. ALDRICH.

Penelope's Suitors. 24mo, boards, 50 cents.
Damen's Ghost. 16mo, $1.00; paper, 50 cents.

Helen Campbell.

Under Green Apple - Boughs. Illustrated. 16mo, paper, 50 cents.

Alice Cary.

Pictures of Country Life. Short Stories. 12mo, $1.50.

Mrs. L. W. Champney.

Rosemary and Rue. 16mo, $1.00.

Clara Erskine Clement.

Eleanor Maitland. 16mo, $1.25; paper, 50 cents.

Mary Clemmer.

His Two Wives. 12mo, $1.50; paper, 50 cents.

An absorbing love story — a portrayal of life held amenable to the lofty and poetic ideal. — *Boston Traveller.*

John Esten Cooke.

Fanchette. 16mo, $1.00.

My Lady Pokahontas. 16mo, gilt top, $1.25.

The narrative of Pokahontas has never been so deliciously presented. — *Quebec Chronicle.*

Rose Terry Cooke.

Somebody's Neighbors. Stories. 12mo, $1.50; half calf, $3.00.

Happy Dodd. 12mo, $1.50.

The Sphinx's Children. Stories. 12mo, $1.50.

Steadfast. 12mo, $1.50.

James Fenimore Cooper.

Works. New *Household Edition.* With Introductions to many of the volumes by Susan Fenimore Cooper, and Illustrations. In 32 volumes. Each, 16mo, $1.00; the set, $32.00; half calf, $64.00.

Precaution.	Wept of Wish-ton-Wish.
The Spy.	The Water-Witch.
The Pioneers.	The Bravo.
The Pathfinder.	Red Rover.
Mercedes of Castile.	Homeward Bound.
The Deerslayer.	Home as Found.
The Red Skins.	The Heidenmauer.
The Chainbearer.	The Headsman.
Satanstoe.	The Two Admirals.
The Crater.	The Pilot.
Afloat and Ashore.	Lionel Lincoln.
The Prairie.	Last of the Mohicans.

Wing and Wing.
Wyandotté.
The Monikins.
Miles Wallingford.

Jack Tier.
The Sea Lions.
Oak Openings.
Ways of the Hour.

New Edition. With Portrait, Illustrations, and Introductions. In 32 vols. 16mo, $32.00. (*Sold only in sets.*)

Fireside Edition. With Portrait, Introductions, and 43 Illustrations. In 16 vols. 12mo, $20.00; half calf, $40.00. (*Sold only in sets.*)

Sea Tales. First Series. New *Household Edition.* With Introductions by Susan Fenimore Cooper. Illustrated. In 5 volumes, the set, 16mo, $5.00; half calf, $10.00.

Sea Tales. Second Series. New *Household Edition.* With Introductions by Susan Fenimore Cooper. Illustrated. In 5 volumes, the set, 16mo, $5.00; half calf, $10.00.

Leather Stocking Tales. New *Household Edition.* With Portrait, Introductions, and Illustrations. In 5 vols., the set, 16mo, $5.00; half calf, $10.00.

Cooper Stories. Narratives of Adventure selected from Cooper's Works. Illustrated. Stories of the Prairie. Stories of the Woods. Stories of the Sea. 3 vols. 16mo, $1.00 each; the set, $3.00.

The Spy. 16mo, paper, 50 cents.

Charles Egbert Craddock [Mary N. Murfree].

In the Tennessee Mountains. Short Stories. 16mo, $1.25.

Mr. Craddock is a master of the art of description. . . . The style is admirable. — *The Nation* (New York).

Down the Ravine. For Young People. Illustrated. 16mo, $1.00.

The Prophet of the Great Smoky Mountains. 16mo, $1.25.

In the Clouds. 16mo, $1.25.

The Story of Keedon Bluffs. 16mo, $1.00.

The Despot of Broomsedge Cove. 16mo, $1.25.

The essential part, the treatment of the human problem, is characterized by real power, — the power of divining motives and piercing through contradictions. Not the hero of " Where the Battle was Fought " is so intensely vital a study as Teck Jepson. The side-lights are not the least striking elements in Miss Murfree's art. — *Springfield Republican.*

Where the Battle was Fought. 16mo, $1.25.

Thomas Frederick Crane (translator).

Italian Popular Tales. With Introduction, Bibliography, Notes, etc. 8vo, gilt top, $2.50.

F. Marion Crawford.

To Leeward. 16mo, $1.25.

A Roman Singer. 16mo, $1.25 ; paper, 50 cents.

An American Politician. 16mo, $1.25.

Paul Patoff. Crown 8vo, $1.50.

Maria S. Cummins.

The Lamplighter. New *Popular Edition.* 12mo, $1.00 ; paper, 25 cents.

El Fureidîs. A Story of Palestine and Syria. 12mo, $1.50 ; paper, 50 cents.

Mabel Vaughan. 12mo, $1.50.

Czeika.

An Operetta in Profile. 16mo, $1.00.

Madeleine Vinton Dahlgren.

A Washington Winter. 12mo, $1.50.

The Lost Name. 12mo, $1.00.

Lights and Shadows of a Life. 12mo, $1.50.

Katharine Floyd Dana.
Our Phil, and other Stories.　Illustrated.
16mo, gilt top, $1.25.

All so true to life, so simple, touching, and so real, as to be as noteworthy from an artistic as well as from a human standpoint. — *New Haven Palladium.*

Parke Danforth.
Not in the Prospectus.　16mo, $1.25.

Charming in style, . . . and altogether as happy a story as we have read for a long time. — *New York Times.*

Daniel De Foe.
Robinson Crusoe.　Illustrated.　12mo, $1.00.

Margaret Deland.
John Ward, Preacher.　55th Thousand.　12mo, $1.50 ; paper, 50 cents.

There are pages in it which, in their power of insight and skill in minute delineation, remind us of Thackeray; while the pictures of country life constantly recall Mrs. Gaskell's fresh and charming tale of "Cranford." — ARCHDEACON FARRAR.

Sidney.　16mo, $1.25.

P. Deming.
Adirondack Stories.　18mo, 75 cents.

Tompkins, and other Folks.　18mo, $1.00.

There is a deep and wonderful art in these quiet little tales. — *The Critic* (New York).

Thomas De Quincey.
Romances and Extravaganzas.　12mo, $1.50.

Narrative and Miscellaneous Papers.　12mo, $1.50.

Charles Dickens.
Complete Works.　*Illustrated Library Edition.*　With Introductions, biographical and historical,

by E. P. Whipple. Containing all the Illustrations that appeared in the English edition by Cruikshank, John Leech, and others, engraved on steel, and the designs of F. O. C. Darley and John Gilbert, in all over 550. In 29 volumes, each, 12mo, $1.50; the set, with Dickens Dictionary, 30 volumes, $45.00; half calf, $82.50; half calf, gilt top, $85.00.

Pickwick Papers, 2 vols.
Nicholas Nickleby, 2 vols.
Oliver Twist, 1 vol.
Old Curiosity Shop, and Reprinted Pieces, 2 vols.
Barnaby Rudge, and Hard Times, 2 vols.
Pictures from Italy, and American Notes, 1 vol.
Bleak House, 2 vols.
Little Dorrit, 2 vols.
David Copperfield, 2 vols.
Martin Chuzzlewit, 2 vols.
Our Mutual Friend, 2 vols.
The Uncommercial Traveller, 1 vol.
A Child's History of England, and other Pieces, 1 vol.
Christmas Books, 1 vol.
Dombey and Son, 2 vols.
Tale of Two Cities, 1 vol.
Great Expectations, 1 vol.
Mystery of Edwin Drood, Master Humphrey's Clock, and other Pieces, 1 vol.
Sketches by Boz, 1 vol.

A Christmas Carol. With thirty Illustrations. 8vo, full flexible leather, $2.00; morocco or tree calf, $7.50. 32mo, 75 cents; paper, 25 cents.

Christmas Books. Illustrated. 12mo, full gilt, $2.00; morocco, $4.50.

Charlotte Dunning.

A Step Aside. 16mo, $1.25; paper, 50 cents.

The *London Saturday Review* said of it: " Miss Dunning's name is new to English readers, but we hope it will not remain so long. She contrives to tell a very unobtrusive story with interest and charm."

Edgar Fawcett.

A Hopeless Case. 18mo, $1.25.

We know of no English novel of the last few years fit to be compared with it in its own line for simplicity, truth, and rational interest. — *London Times.*

A Gentleman of Leisure. 18mo, $1.00.

An Ambitious Woman. Crown 8vo, $1.50 ; paper, 50 cents.

Olivia Delaplaine. 12mo, $1.50.

The Confessions of Claud. 12mo, $1.50 ; paper, 50 cents.

The House at High Bridge. 12mo, $1.50 ; paper, 50 cents.

The Adventures of a Widow. 12mo, $1.50 ; paper, 50 cents.

Tinkling Cymbals. 12mo, $1.50.

Social Silhouettes. 12mo, $1.50.

Mrs. James A. Field.

High-Lights. 16mo, $1.25.

The style and tone of the book quite lift the familiar material out of the ruts, and it is pleasant to record so refined a story. — *The Critic* (New York).

Harford Flemming.

A Carpet Knight. 16mo, $1.25.

Admirably written, with a dash of humor. — *Cleveland Leader.*

Mary Hallock Foote.

The Led-Horse Claim. Illustrated. 16mo, $1.25 ; paper, 50 cents.

John Bodewin's Testimony. 12mo, $1.50 ; paper, 50 cents.

The Last Assembly Ball, and The Fate of a Voice. 16mo, $1.25.

Baron de la Motte Fouqué.

Undine.   18mo, paper, 25 cents.

Undine ; Sintram and His Companions, etc. Illustrated.   32mo, 75 cents.

Undine, and other Tales.   Illustrated.   16mo, $1.00 ; half calf, $2.00.

Johann Wolfgang von Goethe.

Wilhelm Meister.   Translated by Carlyle. With Portrait.   2 vols. crown 8vo, gilt top, $3.00.

The Tale, and Favorite Poems.   Illustrated. 32mo, 75 cents.

Oliver Goldsmith.

The Vicar of Wakefield.   Illustrated.   16mo, $1.00 ; half calf, $2.00.

Handy-Volume Edition.   24mo, gilt top, $1.00.

Jeanie T. Gould [Mrs. Lincoln].

Marjorie's Quest.   For Young People.   Illustrated.   12mo, $1.50.

Her Washington Season.   12mo, $1.50.

Robert Grant.

An Average Man.   12mo, $1.50.

The Confessions of a Frivolous Girl.   12mo, $1.25 ; paper, 50 cents.

A screaming success. — *Saturday Review* (London).

The Knave of Hearts.   12mo, $1.25.

A Romantic Young Lady.   12mo, $1.50.

Henry Gréville.

Cleopatra.   A Russian Romance.   With Portrait of the author.   16mo, $1.25.

Dosia's Daughter.   16mo, $1.25.

Count Xavier.   16mo, $1.00.

Henry Gréville is idyllic, in the sense that most of her stories may be read with pleasure by the innocent maiden and the sophisticated man of the world; how many writers of fiction in these days have been able to attract so diverse an audience? — *Literary Wor".*"(Boston).

The Guardians.

16mo, $1.25.

It is an unusually clever book, every page of which is to be enjoyed, perhaps we may venture to say delighted in. The style is admirable, fresh, crisp, rapid. — *Boston Advertiser.*

Lucretia P. Hale and E. L. Bynner.

An Uncloseted Skeleton. 32mo, boards, 50 cents.

Thomas Chandler Haliburton.

The Clockmaker; or, the Sayings and Doings of Samuel Slick of Slickville. Illustrated. 16mo, $1.00; half calf, $2.00.

Kate W. Hamilton.

Rachel's Share of the Road. 16mo, $1.00.

Mrs. Henrietta Hammond.

The Georgians. 16mo, $1.00.

Arthur Sherburne Hardy.

But Yet a Woman. 16mo, $1.25 ; paper, 50 cents.

The author's drawing of character is the drawing of a master. — *The Academy* (London).

The Wind of Destiny. 16mo, $1.25 ; paper, cents.

Passe Rose. 16mo, $1.25.

Joel Chandler Harris.

Mingo, and other Sketches in Black and White. 16mo, $1.25 ; paper, 50 cents.

Nights with Uncle Remus. Illustrated. 12mo, $1.50 ; paper, 50 cents.

Baalam and his Master.   Short Stories.

Miriam Coles Harris.

Writings.   New Edition, uniform.   Each volume, 16mo, $1.25.   The set, 10 vols, $12.00.

Rutledge.	Frank Warrington.
The Sutherlands.	Richard Vandermarck.
St. Philip's.	Missy.
Happy-Go-Lucky.	Phœbe.
A Perfect Adonis.	

Louie's Last Term at St. Mary's (for Young People).   16mo, $1.00.

Bret Harte.

The Luck of Roaring Camp, and other Sketches.   16mo, $1.25.

The Luck of Roaring Camp, and other Stories.   In Riverside Aldine Series.   16mo, $1.00.
These volumes are not identical in contents.

Mrs. Skaggs's Husbands, etc.   16mo, $1.25.

Tales of the Argonauts, etc.   16mo, $1.25.

Thankful Blossom.   18mo, $1.00.

Two Men of Sandy Bar.   A Play.   18mo, $1.00.

The Story of a Mine.   18mo, $1.00.

Drift from Two Shores.   18mo, $1.00.

The Twins of Table Mountain.   18mo, $1.00.

Flip, and Found at Blazing Star.   18mo, $1.00.

In the Carquinez Woods.   18mo, $1.00.

On the Frontier.   Stories.   18mo, $1.00.

Works.   *Riverside Edition*, rearranged.   With

Portrait and Introduction. In 6 vols., crown 8vo, each $2.00. The set, $12.00; half calf, $18.00; half calf, gilt top, $19.50.

1. Poetical Works, Two Men of Sandy Bar, Introduction, and Portrait. 2. The Luck of Roaring Camp, and other Stories, a portion of the Tales of the Argonauts, etc. 3. Tales of the Argonauts and Eastern Sketches. 4. Gabriel Conroy. 5. Stories, and Condensed Novels. 6. Frontier Stories.

By Shore and Sedge. 18mo, $1.00.

Maruja. 18mo, $1.00.

Snow-Bound at Eagle's. 18mo, $1.00.

A Millionaire of Rough-and-Ready, and Devil's Ford. 18mo, $1.00.

A Phyllis of the Sierras, and Drift from Redwood Camp. 18mo, $1.00.

The Argonauts of North Liberty. 18mo, $1.00.

A Waif of the Plains. 18mo, $1.00.

Novels and Tales. 15 vols., 18mo, $13.00.

Cressy. 16mo, $1.25.

The Crusade of the Excelsior. Illustrated. 16mo, $1.25.

The Heritage of Dedlow Marsh, etc. 16mo, $1.25.

A Ward of the Golden Gate. 16mo, $1.25.

A Sappho of Green Springs. Stories.

Wilhelm Hauff.

Arabian Days' Entertainments. Translated by Herbert Pelham Curtis. Illustrated by Hoppin. New Edition. 12mo, $1.50.

Julian Hawthorne.

Love — or a Name. 12mo, $1.50.

Fortune's Fool. 12mo, $1.50; paper, 50 cents.

Dust. 16mo, paper, 50 cents.

Nathaniel Hawthorne.

Works. *Little Classic Edition.* Each volume contains vignette illustration. In 25 volumes (including Index), 18mo, each $1.00 ; the set, in box, $25.00 ; half calf, $50.00 ; half morocco, gilt top, $62.50 ; tree calf, $75.00.

Twice-Told Tales. 2 vols.
The Snow-Image, and other Twice-Told Tales.
Mosses from an Old Manse. 2 vols.
The Scarlet Letter.
True Stories from History and Biography.
A Wonder-Book for Girls and Boys.
Tanglewood Tales.
American Note-Books. 2 vols.
English Note-Books. 2 vols.
The House of the Seven Gables.
The Blithedale Romance.
The Marble Faun. 2 vols.
Our Old Home. English Sketches.
French and Italian Note-Books. **2 vols.**
Septimius Felton.
Fanshawe, and other Pieces.
The Dolliver Romance, etc.
Sketches and Studies.
Index, and Sketch of Life.

Riverside Edition. With Introductory Notes by George P. Lathrop. With 12 original full-page Etchings and 13 vignette Woodcuts and Portrait. In 13 volumes. Crown 8vo, gilt top, $2.00 each ; the set, $26.00 ; half calf, $39.00 ; half calf, gilt top, $40.50 ; half levant, $52.00.

Twice-Told Tales.
Mosses from an Old Manse.
The House of the Seven Gables, and the Snow-Image.
A Wonder-Book, Tanglewood Tales, etc.
The Scarlet Letter, and The Blithedale Romance.
The Marble Faun.

One Summer. New *Popular Edition.* Illustrated by Hoppin. 16mo, $1.25.

Aulnay Tower. 12mo, $1.50 ; paper, 50 cents.

> A story which, for absorbing interest, brilliancy of style, charm of graphic character drawing, and even exquisite literary quality, will hold its rank among the best work in American fiction. — *Boston Traveller.*

Aunt Serena. 16mo, $1.25 ; paper, 50 cents.

Guenn. Illustrated. 12mo, $1.50; paper, 50 cents.

E. W. Howe.

A Man Story. 12mo, $1.50.

The Mystery of the Locks. New Edition. 16mo, $1.25.

The Story of a Country Town. 12mo, $1.50; paper, 50 cents.

A Moonlight Boy. With Portrait of the Author. 12mo, $1.50; paper, 50 cents.

> Mr. Howe is the strongest man in fiction that the great West has yet produced. — *Boston Transcript.*

William Dean Howells.

Their Wedding Journey. Illustrated. New Edition, with additional chapter. 12mo, $1.50; 18mo, $1.00.

A Chance Acquaintance. Illustrated. 12mo, $1.50 ; 18mo, $1.00.

Suburban Sketches. Illustrated. 12mo, $1.50.

A Foregone Conclusion. 12mo, $1.50.

The Lady of the Aroostook. 12mo, $1.50; paper, 50 cents.

The Undiscovered Country. 12mo, $1.50.

A Day's Pleasure, etc. 32mo, 75 cents; *School Edition*, 40 cents, *net.*

The Minister's Charge. 12mo, $1.50; paper, 50 cents.

Indian Summer. 12mo, $1.50; paper, 50 cents.

The Rise of Silas Lapham. 12mo, $1.50; paper, 50 cents.

A Fearful Responsibility, etc. 12mo, $1.50; paper, 50 cents.

A Modern Instance. 12mo, $1.50; paper, 50 cents.

A Woman's Reason. 12mo, $1.50; paper, 50 cents.

Dr. Breen's Practice. 12mo, $1.50; paper, 50 cents.

The Sleeping-Car, and other Farces. 12mo, $1.00.

The Elevator. 32mo, 50 cents.

The Sleeping-Car. 32mo, 50 cents.

The Parlor Car. 32mo, 50 cents.

The Register. 32mo, 50 cents.

A Counterfeit Presentment. A Comedy. 18mo, $1.25.

Out of the Question. A Comedy. 18mo, $1.25.

A Sea Change; or, Love's Stowaway. A Lyricated Farce. 18mo, $1.00.

Thomas Hughes.

Tom Brown's School Days at Rugby. New Edition. Illustrated. 16mo, $1.00.

Tom Brown at Oxford. 16mo, $1.25.

Henry James.

Watch and Ward. 18mo, $1.25.

A Passionate Pilgrim, and other Tales. 12mo, $2.00.

Roderick Hudson.   12mo, $2.00.

The American.   12mo, $2.00.

The Europeans.   12mo, $1.50.

Confidence.   12mo, $1.50 ; paper, 50 cents.

The Portrait of a Lady.   12mo, $2.00.

The Author of Beltraffio ; Pandora ; Georgina's Reasons ; Four Meetings, etc.   12mo, $1.50.

The Siege of London ; The Pension Beaurepas ; and The Point of View.   12mo, $1.50.

Tales of Three Cities (The Impressions of a Cousin ; Lady Barberina ; A New-England Winter).   12mo, $1.50 ; paper, 50 cents.

Daisy Miller : A Comedy.   12mo, $1.50.

The Tragic Muse.   2 vols. 16mo, $2.50.

Anna Jameson.

Diary of an Ennuyée.   16mo, gilt top, $1.25.

Studies and Stories.   16mo, gilt top, $1.25.

Mrs. C. V. Jamison.

The Story of an Enthusiast.   Told by Himself.   12mo, $1.50 ; paper, 50 cents.

Douglas Jerrold.

Mrs. Caudle's Curtain Lectures.   Illustrated.   16mo, $1.00 ; half calf, $2.00.

Sarah Orne Jewett.

The King of Folly Island, and other People.   16mo, $1.25.

Tales of New England.   In Riverside Aldine Series.   16mo, $1.00.

A White Heron, and other Stories. 18mo, gilt top, $1.25.

A Marsh Island. 16mo, $1.25; paper, 50 cts.

A Country Doctor. 16mo, $1.25.

Deephaven. 18mo, gilt top, $1.25.

Old Friends and New. 18mo, gilt top, $1.25.

Country By-Ways. 18mo, gilt top, $1.25.

The Mate of the Daylight, and Friends Ashore. 18mo, gilt top, $1.25.

Betty Leicester. 18mo, gilt top, $1.25.

Strangers and Wayfarers. 16mo, $1.25.

Rossiter Johnson (editor).

Little Classics. Each in one volume. New Edition, bound in new and artistic style. 18mo, each $1.00. The set, in box, $18.00; half calf, or half morocco, $35.00.

1. Exile.	7. Romance.	13. Narrative Poems.
2. Intellect.	8. Mystery.	14. Lyrical Poems.
3. Tragedy.	9. Comedy.	15. Minor Poems.
4. Life.	10. Childhood.	16. Nature.
5. Laughter.	11. Heroism.	17. Humanity.
6. Love.	12. Fortune.	18. Authors.

A list of the entire contents of the volumes of this Series will be sent free on application.

Virginia W. Johnson.

The House of the Musician. 16mo, paper, 50 cents.

Charles C. Jones, Jr.

Negro Myths from the Georgia Coast. 16mo, $1.00.

Edward King.

The Golden Spike. 12mo, $1.50.

Mr. King is a writer whom we shall look out for; and now that Tourguéneff is dead, it may fall to him to take up the mantle of the prophet. — *The Literary World* (London).

The Gentle Savage.   12mo, $2.00.

Ellen Olney Kirk.

The Story of Margaret Kent.   New Edition. 16mo, $1.25 ; paper, 50 cents.

In "The Story of Margaret Kent" we have that rare thing in current literature, *a really good novel*. . . . Aside from the other merits which we have noted, this novel is to be praised for its artistic earnestness and sincerity. — *Boston Advertiser.*

Sons and Daughters.   12mo, $1.50 ; paper, 50 cents.

Queen Money.   New Edition.   16mo, $1.25 ; paper, 50 cents.

Better Times.   Stories.   12mo, $1.50.

A Midsummer Madness.   16mo, $1.25.

A Lesson in Love.   16mo, $1.00 ; paper, 50 cents.

A Daughter of Eve.   12mo, $1.50 ; paper, 50 cents.

Walford.   16mo, $1.25.

Joseph Kirkland.

Zury: The Meanest Man in Spring County. A Novel of Western Life.   With Frontispiece.   12mo, $1.50 ; paper, 50 cents.

The McVeys.   16mo, $1.25.

Charles and Mary Lamb.

Tales from Shakespeare.   18mo, $1.00.

Handy-Volume Edition.   24mo, gilt top, $1.00.

The Same.   Illustrated.   16mo, $1.00.

Mary Catherine Lee.

A Quaker Girl of Nantucket.   16mo, $1.25.

In the Cheering-Up Business.   16mo, $1.25.

Henry Wadsworth Longfellow.

Hyperion.   A Romance.   16mo, $1.50.

Popular Edition.   16mo, 40 cents; paper, 15 cents.

Outre-Mer.   16mo, $1.50.

Popular Edition.   16mo, 40 cents; paper, 15 cents.

Kavanagh.   A Romance.   16mo, $1.50.

Hyperion, Outre-Mer, and Kavanagh.   In 2 volumes, crown 8vo, $3.00.

Flora Haines Loughead.

The Man who was Guilty.   16mo, $1.25.

It is earnest, high-minded, and moving, lighted here and there by a demure drollery, interesting as a story, and provocative of serious thought. — *Overland Monthly* (San Francisco).

Madame Lucas.

16mo, $1.00; paper, 50 cents.

D. R. McAnally.

Irish Wonders: The Ghosts, Giants, Pookas, Demons, Leprechawns, Banshees, Fairies, Witches, Widows, Old Maids, and other Marvels of the Emerald Isle.   Popular Tales as told by the People. Profusely illustrated.   Square 8vo, $2.00.

S. Weir Mitchell.

In War Time.   16mo, $1.25; paper, 50 cents.

Roland Blake.   16mo, $1.25.

Dr. Mitchell's book is indeed one to be grateful for. It is interpenetrated by fine and true shades of thought, and worked out

with delicacy and artistic feeling. It contains striking, even brilliant incidents, yet its interest depends chiefly upon modifications
of character. — *American* (Philadelphia).

Luigi Monti.

Leone. 16mo, $1.00 ; paper, 50 cents.

A story of Italian life written by an Italian, and shows an im-
pressive fidelity to time and place. — *Boston Traveller.*

Henry L. Nelson.

John Rantoul. 12mo, $1.50.

Mrs. Oliphant and T. B. Aldrich.

The Second Son. Crown 8vo, $1.50 ; paper,
50 cents.

Peppermint Perkins.

The Familiar Letters of Peppermint Perkins.
Illustrated. 16mo, $1.00 ; paper, 50 cents.

Nora Perry.

The Youngest Miss Lorton, and other Stories.
Illustrated. 12mo, $1.50.

A Flock of Girls. Stories. Illustrated. 12mo,
$1.50.
For a Woman. 18mo, $1.00.
A Book of Love Stories. 16mo, $1.00.
The Tragedy of the Unexpected. 18mo,
$1.25.

Elizabeth Stuart Phelps [Mrs. Ward].

The Gates Ajar. 75th Thousand. 16mo,
$1.50.
Beyond the Gates. 16mo, $1.25.
The Gates Between. 16mo, $1.25.

The above three volumes, in box, $4.00.

Men, Women, and Ghosts. Stories. 16mo, $1.50.

Hedged In. 16mo, $1.50.

The Silent Partner. 16mo, $1.50.

The Story of Avis. 16mo, $1.50; paper, 50 cents.

Sealed Orders, and other Stories. 16mo, $1.50.

Friends: A Duet. 16mo, $1.25.

Doctor Zay. 16mo, $1.25; paper, 50 cents.

An Old Maid's Paradise, and Burglars in Paradise. 16mo, $1.25.

The Master of the Magicians. Collaborated by Elizabeth Stuart Phelps and Herbert D. Ward. 16mo, $1.25.

Come Forth. Collaborated by Elizabeth Stuart Phelps and Herbert D. Ward. 16mo, $1.25.

The above thirteen volumes, $17.50.

The Madonna of the Tubs. With Illustrations. 12mo, full gilt, $1.50.

Jack the Fisherman. Illustrated. Square 12mo, ornamental boards, 50 cents.

Melville Philips.

The Devil's Hat. 16mo, $1.00.

Eça de Queiros.

Dragon's Teeth. Translated from the Portuguese by Mary J. Serrano. 12mo, $1.50.

Edmund Quincy.

The Haunted Adjutant; and other Stories. 12mo, $1.50.

Wensley; and other Stories. 12mo, $1.50.

J. P. Quincy.
The Peckster Professorship. 16mo, $1.25.

Opie P. Read.
Len Gansett. 16mo, $1.00; paper, 50 cents.

Marian C. L. Reeves and Emily Read.
Pilot Fortune. 16mo, $1.25.

A Reverend Idol.
A Novel. 12mo, $1.50; paper, 50 cents.

Riverside Paper Series.
A Continuation of Ticknor's Paper Series, appearing semi-monthly during the summer. Each, 16mo, paper, 50 cents.

1. John Ward, Preacher. By Margaret Deland.
2. The Scarlet Letter. By Nathaniel Hawthorne.
3. But Yet a Woman. By A. S. Hardy.
4. The Queen of Sheba. By T. B. Aldrich.
5. The Story of Avis. By Elizabeth Stuart Phelps.
6. The Feud of Oakfield Creek. By Josiah Royce.
7. Agatha Page. By Isaac Henderson.
8. The Guardian Angel. By Oliver Wendell Holmes.
9. A Step Aside. By Charlotte Dunning.
10. An Ambitious Woman. By Edgar Fawcett.
11. The Spy. By James Fenimore Cooper.
12. Emerson's Essays. First and Second Series.
13. In War Time. By Dr. S. Weir Mitchell.
14. Elsie Venner. By Dr. O. W. Holmes.
15. Agnes of Sorrento. By Harriet Beecher Stowe.
16. The Lady of the Aroostook. By W. D. Howells.
17. A Roman Singer. By F. Marion Crawford.
18. The Second Son. By Mrs. Oliphant and T. B. Aldrich.
19. A Daughter of Eve. By Ellen Olney Kirk.

20. A Marsh Island. By Sarah O. Jewett.
21. The Wind of Destiny. By A. S. Hardy.
22. A Lesson in Love. By Ellen Olney Kirk.
23. El Fureidîs. By Maria S. Cummins.
24. The Fate of Mansfield Humphreys. By Richard Grant White.
25. Prudence Palfrey. By T. B. Aldrich.
26. The Golden Justice. By W. H. Bishop.
27. Doctor Zay. By E. S. Phelps.
28. Zury. By Joseph Kirkland.
29. Confidence. By Henry James.
30. Young Maids and Old. Clara L. Burnham.

Extra Number 3. Ein Rückblick. (Looking Backward.) Translated into German by Rabbi Solomon Schindler.

Extra Number 5. Mosses from an Old Manse. By Nathaniel Hawthorne.

Extra Number 8. Looking Backward, 2000–1887. By Edward Bellamy. New Edition. 371st Thousand.

Other numbers to be announced later.

Edith Robinson.

Forced Acquaintances. 12mo, $1.50 ; paper, 50 cents.

Round-Robin Series.

Each volume, 16mo, $1.00; paper, 50 cents.

Damen's Ghost.	The Strike in the B—— Mill.
Madame Lucas.	Rosemary and Rue.
Leone.	Fanchette.
Doctor Ben.	Dorothea.

N. B. *The last three can be had in cloth only.*

Josiah Royce.

The Feud of Oakfield Creek. A Novel of California. 16mo, $1.25 ; paper, 50 cents.

Joseph Xavier Boniface Saintine.

Picciola. Illustrated. 16mo, $1.00 ; half calf, $2.00.

J. H. Bernardin de Saint-Pierre.

Paul and Virginia. Illustrated. 16mo, $1.00.
The Same, together with Undine and Sintram.
Illustrated. 32mo, 75 cents ; *School Edition*, 40 cents.

Sir Walter Scott.

The Waverley Novels. *Illustrated Library Edition.* Illustrated with 100 Engravings by famous artists ; and with Introductions, Illustrative Notes, Glossary, and Index of Characters. In 25 volumes, 12mo. Each, $1.00 ; the set, $25.00 ; half calf, $50.00 ; half calf, gilt top, $55.00.

Waverley.	The Fortunes of Nigel.
Guy Mannering.	Peveril of the Peak.
The Antiquary.	Quentin Durward.
Rob Roy.	St. Ronan's Well.
Old Mortality.	Redgauntlet.
Black Dwarf, and The Legend of Montrose.	The Betrothed, and The Highland Widow.
Heart of Mid-Lothian.	The Talisman and other Tales.
The Bride of Lammermoor.	
Ivanhoe.	Woodstock.
The Monastery.	The Fair Maid of Perth.
The Abbot.	Anne of Geierstein.
Kenilworth.	Count Robert of Paris.
The Pirate.	The Surgeon's Daughter, and Castle Dangerous.

Horace E. Scudder.

The Dwellers in Five-Sisters' Court. 16mo, $1.25.
Stories and Romances. 16mo, $1.25.

Mark Sibley Severance.

Hammersmith ; His Harvard Days. 12mo, $1.50.

We do not recall any other book which so well deserves to be associated with the " Tom Brown " stories. — *Boston Journal.*

J. Emerson Smith.

Oakridge: An Old-Time Story of Maine.
12mo, $2.00.

Mary A. Sprague.

An Earnest Trifler. 16mo, $1.25.

Willis Steell.

Isidra. A Mexican Novel. 12mo, $1.25.

A. Stirling.

At Daybreak. 16mo, $1.25.

Louise Stockton.

Dorothea. 16mo, $1.00.

William W. Story.

Fiammetta: A Summer Idyl. 16mo, $1.25.

Harriet Beecher Stowe.

Uncle Tom's Cabin. A Story of Slavery.
Illustrated. 12mo, $2.00.

Illustrated Holiday Edition. With Introduction and Bibliography and over 100 Illustrations. 8vo, full gilt, $3.00; half calf, $5.00; levant, or tree calf, $6.00.

New *Popular Edition*, from new plates. With Account of the writing of this Story by Mrs. Stowe, and Frontispiece. 16mo, $1.00.

"Uncle Tom's Cabin" . . . must always remain one of the monuments of literature. — *New York Evening Post.*

Agnes of Sorrento. 12mo, $1.50; paper, 50 cents.

The Pearl of Orr's Island. 12mo, $1.50.

The Minister's Wooing. 12mo, $1.50.

My Wife and I.   Illustrated.   12mo, $1.50.

We and our Neighbors.   A Sequel to My Wife and I.   New Edition.   Illustrated.   12mo, $1.50.

Poganuc People.   Illustrated.   12mo, $1.50.

The May-Flower, and other Sketches.   12mo, $1.50.

Dred.   (Nina Gordon.)   New Edition.   12mo, $1.50.

Oldtown Folks.   12mo, $1.50.

Sam Lawson's Fireside Stories.   Illustrated. New Edition, enlarged.   12mo, $1.50.

The above eleven 12mo volumes, in box, $16.00.

Strike in the B—— Mill, The.

16mo, $1.00; paper, 50 cents.

Mary P. Thacher.

Sea-shore and Prairie.   Stories and Sketches. 18mo, $1.00.

William Makepeace Thackeray.

Complete Works.   *Illustrated Library Edition.*   Including two newly compiled volumes, containing material not hitherto collected in any American or English Edition.   With Biographical and Bibliographical Introductions, Portrait, and over 1600 Illustrations.   22 vols. crown 8vo, each, $1.50.   The set, $33.00; half calf, $60.50; half calf, gilt top, $65.00; half levant, $77.00.

1. Vanity Fair. I.
2. Vanity Fair. II.; Lovel the Widower.
3. Pendennis. I.
4. Pendennis. II.
5. Memoirs of Yellowplush.
6. Burlesques, etc.
7. History of Samuel Titmarsh, etc.
8. Barry Lyndon and Denis Duval.
9. The Newcomes. I.
10. The Newcomes. II.
11. Paris Sketch Book, etc.

12. Irish Sketch Book, etc.
13. The Four Georges, etc.
14. Henry Esmond.
15. The Virginians. I.
16. The Virginians. II.
17. Philip. I.
18. Philip. II. ; Catherine.
19. Roundabout Papers, etc.
20. Christmas Stories, etc.
21. Contributions to Punch, etc.
22. Miscellaneous Essays.

The Introductory Notes give every interesting detail about the origins and fortunes of separate works that can be gathered from the literature about Thackeray. — *Literary World* (Boston).

Octave Thanet.

Knitters in the Sun. 16mo, $1.25.

The best collection of short stories we have read for many a day. R. H. STODDARD in *New York Mail and Express.*

Frederick Thickstun.

A Mexican Girl. 16mo, $1.25 ; paper, 50 cents.

The sketches of scenery are as true as they are telling, and the character painting is strong and life-like. The racy writing and the abundant flow of humor that constitute so large a part of the charm of the Pacific-coast literature are at high tide in Mr. Thickstun's story. — *Literary World* (London).

Chauncey Thomas.

The Crystal Button ; or, Adventures of Paul Prognosis in the Forty-Ninth Century. Edited by George Houghton. 16mo, $1.25.

Maurice Thompson.

A Tallahassee Girl. 16mo, $1.00 ; paper, 50 cents.

Among the very best of recent American stories, and very far ahead of any of the many novels of Southern life. — *Philadelphia Times.*

Ticknor's Paper Series.

For Leisure-Hour and Railroad Reading.

Each volume, 16mo, paper, 50 cents.

1. The Story of Margaret Kent. By Ellen Olney Kirk.
2. Guenn. By Blanche Willis Howard.
4. A Reverend Idol. A Massachusetts Coast Romance.
5. A Nameless Nobleman. By Jane G. Austin.
6. The Prelate. A Roman Story. By Isaac Henderson.
7. Eleanor Maitland. By Clara Erskine Clement.
8. The House of the Musician. By Virginia W. Johnson.
9. Geraldine. A Metrical Romance of the St. Lawrence.
10. The Duchess Emilia. By Barrett Wendell.
11. Dr. Breen's Practice. By W. D. Howells.
12. Tales of Three Cities. By Henry James.
13. The House at High Bridge. By Edgar Fawcett.
14. The Story of a Country Town. By E. W. Howe.
15. The Confessions of a Frivolous Girl. By Robert Grant.
16. Culture's Garland. By Eugene Field.
17. Patty's Perversities. By Arlo Bates.
18. A Modern Instance. By W. D. Howells.
19. Miss Ludington's Sister. By Edward Bellamy.
20. Aunt Serena. By Blanche Willis Howard.
21. Damen's Ghost. By Edwin Lassetter Bynner.
22. A Woman's Reason. By W. D. Howells.
23. Nights with Uncle Remus. By Joel Chandler Harris.
24. Mingo. By Joel Chandler Harris.
25. A Tallahassee Girl. By Maurice Thompson.
27. A Fearful Responsibility. By W. D. Howells.
28. Homoselle. By Mary S. Tiernan.
29. A Moonlight Boy. By E. W. Howe.
30. Adventures of a Widow. By Edgar Fawcett.
31. Indian Summer. By W. D. Howells.
32. The Led-Horse Claim. By Mary Hallock Foote.
33. Len Gansett. By Opie P. Read.
34. Next Door. By Clara Louise Burnham.

35. The Minister's Charge. By W. D. Howells.
36. Sons and Daughters. By Ellen Olney Kirk.
37. Agnes Surriage. By Edwin Lassetter Bynner.
39. Two College Girls. By Helen Dawes Brown.
40. The Rise of Silas Lapham. By W. D. Howells.
41. A Mexican Girl. By Frederick Thickstun.
42. Aulnay Tower. By Blanche Willis Howard.
43. The Pagans. By Arlo Bates.
44. Fortune's Fool. By Julian Hawthorne.
45. Doctor Ben. By Orlando Witherspoon.
46. John Bodewin's Testimony. By Mary Hallock Foote.
47. Rachel Armstrong; or, Love and Theology. By Celia Parker Woolley.
48. Two Gentlemen of Boston.
49. The Confessions of Claud. By Edgar Fawcett.
50. His Two Wives. By Mary Clemmer.
51. The Desmond Hundred. By Jane G. Austin.
52. A Woman of Honor. By H. C. Bunner.
53. Forced Acquaintances. By Edith Robinson.
54. Under Green Apple-Boughs. By Helen Campbell.
55. Fools of Nature. By Alice Brown.
56. Dust. By Julian Hawthorne.
57. The Story of an Enthusiast. By Mrs. C. V. Jamison.
58. Queen Money. By Ellen Olney Kirk.

There is not a poor novel in the series. I have been asked to give a list of good reading in fiction such as one about to go away can buy. I have no hesitation in naming most of the numbers in this series. — *Boston Advertiser.*

Mary S. Tiernan.
Homoselle. 16mo, $1.00 ; paper, 50 cents.
Jack Horner. 16mo, $1.25.

Mary Agnes Tincker.
Two Coronets. 12mo, $1.50.

Two Gentlemen of Boston.

12mo, $1.50 ; paper, 50 cents.

The writer has three of the best gifts of the novelist — imagination, perception, and humor. — *New York Tribune.*

Gen. Lew Wallace.

The Fair God ; or, The Last of the 'Tzins. A Tale of the Conquest of Mexico. 94th Thousand. 12mo, $1.50.

We do not hesitate to say that the " Fair God " is one of the most powerful historical novels we have ever read. The scene where in the sunrise Montezuma reads his fate, the dance-scene, and the entry of the Spaniards to the capital, are drawn in a style of which we think few living writers capable ; and the battles are Homeric in their grandeur. — *London Athenæum.*

Henry Watterson (editor).

Oddities in Southern Life and Character. With Illustrations by W. L. Sheppard and F. S. Church. 16mo, $1.50.

Kate Gannett Wells.

Miss Curtis. 12mo, $1.25.

As nobody knows Boston social life better than Mrs. Wells, the book is full of deliciously felicitous touches of social satire and wisdom. — ARLO BATES, in *The Book Buyer.*

Barrett Wendell.

Rankell's Remains. 16mo, $1.00.

The Duchess Emilia. 16mo, $1.00 ; paper, 50 cents.

One of the most striking features of this romance of metempsychosis is the delicate poetic feeling with which he has invested it. — *Springfield Republican.*

Richard Grant White.

The Fate of Mansfield Humphreys, with the Episode of Mr. Washington Adams in England. 16mo, $1.25 ; paper, 50 cents.

Bright, full of character, a little satirical, and thoroughly amusing. — *Christian Advocate* (New York).

Mrs. A. D. T. Whitney.

Ascutney Street. 12mo, $1.50.

Faith Gartney's Girlhood. Illustrated. 12mo, $1.50.

Hitherto. 12mo, $1.50.

Patience Strong's Outings. 12mo, $1.50.

The Gayworthys. 12mo, $1.50.

A Summer in Leslie Goldthwaite's Life. Illustrated. 12mo, $1.50.

We Girls. Illustrated. 12mo, $1.50.

Real Folks. Illustrated. 12mo, $1.50.

The Other Girls. Illustrated. 12mo, $1.50.

Sights and Insights. 2 vols. 12mo, $3.00.

Odd or Even ? 12mo, $1.50.

Bonnyborough. 12mo, $1.50.

Homespun Yarns. Stories. 12mo, $1.50.

John Greenleaf Whittier.

Margaret Smith's Journal, Tales, and Sketches. *Riverside Edition.* Crown 8vo, $1.50.

Kate Douglas Wiggin.

Timothy's Quest. 16mo, $1.00.

The Birds' Christmas Carol. With Illustrations. Square 16mo, boards, 50 cents.

The only fault of this charming little book is that there is not enough of it. — *New Haven Palladium.*

The Story of Patsy. Illustrated. Square 16mo, boards, 60 cents.

Justin Winsor.

Was Shakespeare Shapleigh? 16mo, rubricated parchment-paper covers, 75 cents.

Orlando Witherspoon.

Doctor Ben. 16mo, $1.00; paper, 50 cents.

Celia Parker Woolley.

Rachel Armstrong; or, Love and Theology. 12mo, $1.50; paper, 50 cents.

A Girl Graduate. 12mo, $1.50.

A. H. Wratislaw (translator).

Sixty Folk-Tales. From exclusively Slavonic Sources. Crown 8vo, gilt top, $2.00.

Lillie Chace Wyman.

Poverty Grass. Short Stories. 16mo, $1.25.

"Poverty Grass" is much more than a story book: it is a moral deed. Let those who think our social system perfect pause and read. — *Boston Beacon.*

*** For sale by all Booksellers. Sent, post-paid, on receipt of price by the Publishers,*

Houghton, Mifflin & Company,

4 Park Street, Boston; 11 East 17th Street, New York.

www.ingramcontent.com/pod-product-compliance
Lightning Source LLC
Chambersburg PA
CBHW020933030726
47496CB00005B/1170